The Vintage Tea Room

Collection

Books 1-3

Lily Wells

Contents

Book One
The Vintage Tea Room
end of an era and new beginnings

Book Two
The Vintage Tea Room 2
room for a small one

Book Three
The Vintage Tea Room 3
changing times and new opportunities

Lily Wells

Book One

The Vintage Tea Room
end of an era and new beginnings

Lily Wells

Lily Wells

1

Ellie did a final check of the tea room – fresh flowers, clean tablecloths and straight pictures. From the moment she'd bought this place she knew she'd wanted to create a traditional tea room. Vintage but not old fashioned. In an age of wipe clean tables and large mugs she'd gone for tablecloths covered with English flowers, white napkins, cups with saucers, and patterned wallpaper.

She'd arranged for the photographer to come on a Tuesday because she usually had a little more time during the morning, it was still busy but as she did a lot of preparation for the week on a Monday she could almost relax.

She loved this time of day especially when, like today, the morning sun streamed through the windows. Even though the street outside was narrow with shops on both sides it never appeared dark or dingy, the sunlight found its way through and added a brightness to the honey coloured Cotswold stone buildings. With the tables and chairs outside she thought this area almost had a Parisian feel. Ellie took a moment to watch people as they wandered down the street, some on their way to work, others out shopping, and a few tourists looking through their guide books and taking photos as they admired the historic buildings.

Ellie took one last glance before turning back to the job in hand, soon this view would no longer be hers. She turned on the coffee machine behind the counter before going into the adjoining kitchen to turn on the urn. As she collected the cakes from the fridge the bell on the tea room door jingled.

"Hi, is that you Joe," she called out without looking round.

"Who's Joe?" came the reply.

"Jessica, what are you doing here?" Ellie said as she hurried back into the tea room.

"Good to see you too, Mum," Jessica said, "and again, who is Joe?"

"Joe's the photographer, but never mind that, is everything okay?" Ellie said looking at Jessica's tiny bump. She'd been over the moon when she'd heard Jessica was expecting her first baby.

"I'm fine, or rather the baby's fine, I've left Edward and come back here to live," Jessica said as she sat at one of the tables and put her bag on the floor.

"Oh, Jessie," said Ellie putting her arm around her shoulders. "What's happened?"

Before Jessica could answer the doorbell jingled again.

"Hi, Ellie," said a young man with a camera around his neck. "Is now a good time?" he asked looking from Ellie to Jessica. "The office said to come early before you had customers."

"Now's perfect," said Ellie smiling.

Ellie turned back to Jessica. "Give me ten minutes to show Joe around and then I'll make some tea and you can tell me everything."

"Fine," replied Jessica. "I'll take my things up to my room."

"Actually, could you wait in the back room," said Ellie looking a little sheepishly at Jessica. "Joe needs to take some photos upstairs."

Ellie caught the look of annoyance of Jessica's face as she got up and went through to the hallway.

"Sorry about that," Ellie said looking back at Joe. "Unexpected visit."

"No worries," Joe said. "Show me around and then I'll start snapping. I'll start outside since the sun's out. I must say this place has real appeal, I think you'll get a buyer in no time."

"I hope so," said Ellie, "now I've made the decision to sell I'd like to get things moving quickly."

"I think we have a number of people on our books looking for a home and business. They're mostly families hoping to find that dream lifestyle. And, let's face it, you don't get much better than this - Cotswold location, vibrant town, something for all the family, it's the perfect package," said Joe smiling.

"Wow, how could anyone resist," Ellie said laughing.

"I should be able to get some really good shots so lead the way," Joe said.

Ellie led Joe into the kitchen and on through to the office behind. She then doubled back and took him into the hallway that led to the main house which was mainly above the tea room.

To the right of the stairs was a small sitting room, affectionately called the back room, with French doors leading out onto the courtyard. Ellie looked at the closed door, she hoped Jessica would be alright for a few minutes.

"You'd best do this room last," Ellie said. "I need to explain to Jessica first."

Joe followed Ellie upstairs where she gave him a whistle-stop tour of the rooms - kitchen, sitting room, bathroom and four bedrooms. She'd spent the last two weeks sprucing it up a little ready to sell. She'd painted, bought new bed linen and some new rugs. And, of course, did the obligatory de-clutter.

"I'll leave you to it," Ellie said. "You've got about an hour until we open."

"That's plenty of time," Joe said. "I'll find you when I'm done."

2

Ellie went back down to the kitchen and put the kettle on; the water in the urn wasn't yet hot enough to use. She loved the routine of preparing a pot of tea - warming the pot, laying a tray and putting milk, lemon and sugar into the little containers. Twenty-three years ago she might have thought this was a lot of fuss for one cup of tea, now she knew better.

She selected a Breakfast Tea, a perfect pick-me-up in the morning. Ellie put the pot on the tray and carried it through to the back room. Calling this the back room didn't do it justice, it was a pretty, bright room that had served many purposes. Years ago it had been the playroom for the twins and then a room for them to bring their friends when they wanted to be cool and not be too close to their mother. Now it had a sofa, a small wicker and glass dining set and her CD player. She would often sit here when she took a break from work or during the evening, especially in the summer when she opened up the French doors and allowed the warm air to drift into the room.

Jessica was sitting at the table looking out into the courtyard. Ellie followed her gaze towards the large pots of daffodils just outside the doors. Daffodils were one of her favourite flowers, they heralded in the warmer weather even if they often appeared when it was snowing, raining or bitterly cold, and they had that magical ability to make her smile.

"Here you go, Jessica," Ellie said as she put the tray on the table and poured two cups of tea. "Now tell me what's happened."

"I think you'd better tell me what's going on with Joe. Are you being photographed for one of those lifestyle magazines?" asked Jessica.

"Not exactly, I'll explain later. You go first, have you had a row?" asked Ellie.

Jessica let out a sob. "No, I just can't live with him anymore, he's…," she paused, "he's suffocating me," she said.

"What do you mean, I thought you two were great together, I'd never had him down as the possessive type," Ellie said. Edward had always seemed a great guy, reliable, wouldn't do anything to hurt Jessica.

"He's not, it's just that since I got pregnant things have changed," Jessica said.

"How?" asked Ellie.

"Well, every weekend he wants to paint the nursery or look at prams or talk about baby names," Jessica said.

"That doesn't sound too bad," Ellie said, smiling.

"You wouldn't understand," Jessica said.

Ellie could see tears form in the corner of her eyes.

"Try me," Ellie said.

"We used to go out, meet friends, have fun," Jessica said, the tears had started to fall down her cheeks.

"I thought you were pleased about the baby, and it sounds like Edward is really happy too, so what's wrong?" said Ellie.

"I am pleased, but we don't have to spend every spare minute preparing," said Jessica, sobbing.

"Getting ready for the baby is important, but you're right, you do need time to adjust as things will be very different once the baby's born. Maybe it's Edward's way of getting involved, you know, doing his bit to help," said Ellie. She put an arm around her daughter.

"I know I sound selfish, but the baby doesn't have to become our entire focus," said Jessica.

"Trust me, he or she will take up most of your waking hours, at least for the first few months. Have you told Edward how you feel?" Ellie asked.

"No, he'll only tell me that feeling like this is normal and I'll soon get excited about the whole thing," Jessica said. She took a tissue from her bag and wiped her eyes. The tears had stopped and she began to sound a little bit calmer.

"Maybe he's wiser than you think," said Ellie.

"Don't you start, I came here for a bit of support," Jessica said.

"You have told him you're here?" Ellie asked.

"Not yet," Jessica replied looking into her cup.

"You know you're welcome to stay for as long as you like but you do need to tell him where you are, it's not fair to let him worry," Ellie said.

"I'll text him later, he'll be busy now," Jessica said. "And he won't know I'm gone until he gets home tonight."

"Don't you think he deserves a phone call," Ellie said gently, trying to avoid upsetting Jessica again.

"I guess, but I don't want to hear him fussing," Jessica said.

Ellie sipped her tea and stared at the little roses around the top of the cup. When she'd first arrived in Cirencester the only thing she knew about tea was how to put a teabag into a mug and yet she'd decided tea was going to be her speciality and the little café she had bought was going to be a proper tea room. She'd read books, visited tea merchants, attended fairs, tasted samples and even visited a plantation in Africa. Eventually she felt she had a pretty reasonable knowledge of the different teas and blends. Her customers could choose from a good selection from across the world and, if needed, she could offer them advice. Despite the growing trend for coffee shops, several had opened in the town and were very popular, her tea room had kept its customers and attracted the tourists. During the summer it was usually full and even in winter she was kept busy.

"Your turn mum," Jessica said breaking into her thoughts. "What's going on with Joe?"

"He's from the estate agent, he's taking the photos for the brochure," Ellie replied.

"What brochure?" Jessica asked putting her cup down and looking directly at Ellie.

Ellie looked at Jessica, she hadn't planned to tell her like this but, as she couldn't avoid it, she might as well just say it.

"I'm selling the tea room," said Ellie.

"Selling, you can't sell, this is our home. When were you going to discuss this with us, or have you already spoken to

Marie, I bet you have, you always tell her everything first just because she's the oldest," Jessica said rushing the words out.

"You're twins born minutes apart so I don't think that counts as older. I was going to tell you both before it goes on the market, probably next week," said Ellie.

"But you can't sell our home," Jessica said.

"It's too big for me and I want to do something different," said Ellie.

"Like what? You're too young to retire," said Jessica.

"I'm not retiring, I just thought I'd try a change of direction that's all," Ellie said, she was a little surprised at Jessica's reaction after all she hadn't lived here for quite some years now and rarely stayed overnight when she did visit.

Joe popped his head into the back room.

"Nearly done," he said. "I'll get some photos of the courtyard then I'll be finished. We'll get the brochure put together and I'll bring a copy across."

"Thanks, go on through," Ellie said.

"You can't really be selling, what will you do?" said Jessica when Joe was out of earshot.

"I'm downsizing, I think that's the fashionable term. I'm going to keep the cake side of the business and run that from the cottage. And I intend to travel, you know all the places I've dreamed of visiting. I'll also be able to see more of you and your sister, as you know it's always been difficult to get away," Ellie said.

"Back up a bit. What cottage?" asked Jessica.

"The one I'm going to buy," said Ellie realising that perhaps she should have told the girls beforehand but, to be honest, she didn't think they'd be that interested. After all they were leading their own lives now.

"This all seems a bit sudden, don't you think you should take some time to think it through properly?" said Jessica.

"It's not that sudden. I saw the cottage a month or so ago, that's what made me decide to sell. Bit of fate really, I was driving to deliver a cake just outside Cirencester and passed this lovely cottage with a for sale sign. As luck would have it the owner was outside and we had a chat. She kindly showed me around and, well the place was perfect so I put in an offer and decided to sell," said Ellie.

"But Mum, this is our family home," Jessica said with a hint of pleading in her voice.

"Both you and your sister moved out a long time ago, it hasn't been a family home for some while. It's time it had a new lease of life. Come on I'll help you with your things, your room's pretty much the same but I have given it a lick of paint. And some of your bits are stored under the bed. A bit of staging can only help the sale," she said laughing.

Jessica looked at her scowling. "I don't think this is anything to laugh about," she said.

Joe came back in from the courtyard so Ellie decided not to respond. Maybe Jessica just needed some time to get used to the idea.

3

Ellie left Jessica resting in her bedroom, the early morning start and train journey from Bristol had left her looking tired. Add to that the shock of learning she was selling the tea room, even though she had been surprised at her reaction, and she probably needed to catch up on her sleep. She had initially been surprised that Jessica hadn't driven up but she'd soon realised that coming here was a bit of a sudden decision and her husband, Edward, had the car. Ellie would need to make sure Jessica got in touch with him, from what Jessica had said he clearly cared about her and didn't even realise Jessica was unhappy.

Ellie went back into the kitchen and put on her apron ready to open up. With the glorious spring weather and less than a week to go before the school holidays the early tourists would be out in force. Pat would be here shortly, it was just the two of them this week as the seasonal staff didn't start until next Monday, just before the Easter weekend.

Pat had been a real godsend when she'd first opened the tea room. Not only did she know how to make a proper pot of tea she also made the most exquisite miniature cakes. The customers loved them, instead of having to choose one large slice of cake, always difficult when they all looked so good, they could select three or four miniatures and try them all. It was when Ellie had first displayed these miniatures on a tiered cake stand that she'd had the idea to offer proper afternoon tea with delicate looking cakes and sandwiches rather than a full lunch menu.

The bell on the door jingled again as Pat came into the tea room. As usual she was dressed in her black trousers and white top. Even though Ellie hadn't initially had a uniform for staff, she'd only insisted on them wearing a white apron, Pat's black and white dress code was adopted by herself and soon became the dress code for all her staff.

"Morning Ellie," said Pat. "Has the photographer

been?"

"Yes," said Ellie, it was a good job Jessica was still upstairs, she'd be really annoyed that Pat knew about the sale. "He says he's got some great shots."

"I'm going to miss you," said Pat as she put on her apron.

"I won't be that far away, and I'll probably pop back in for a quick cuppa," said Ellie.

"I'm not sure I'll be here," said Pat.

"The new owners are bound to want you to stay," Ellie said, "you know this place inside out."

"Maybe, but I'm sure they'll want to put their own stamp on the place and, as you know, I've never been that good with change," Pat said. "I have been thinking about retiring."

"The regulars will miss you. I think some of them come in more for a chat with you than a cup of tea," Ellie said laughing.

With that the first customer of the day arrived. Margaret came in every Tuesday and Thursday, usually as soon as they opened. She lived in one of the villages outside the town and caught the bus in to do her shopping and visit her sister. Ellie always admired the effort Margaret took with her appearance, her grey hair was pinned up, make-up was carefully applied and her clothes were well put together. Ellie had never made that much effort to go shopping.

"Morning Margaret," said Ellie, "your usual?"

"Yes please," said Margaret as she sat at a table next to the window.

Ellie made a pot of Earl Grey tea, laid a tray and carried it across to Margaret.

"The cake's on me," she said indicating a miniature slice of lemon sponge topped with a lemon glaze. "A new recipe, let me know what you think."

"Thank you," said Margaret as she poured the tea into her cup. "If it tastes as good as it looks it'll be a sure fire winner."

Ellie genuinely valued the opinion of her customers,

especially those who came back week after week and kept her in business during the winter. She trusted their comments and if several customers said they didn't think a cake was right for the tea room then she'd take their advice. Some customers even brought in their own recipes for her to try, the idea had become so popular that she now had a customer special cake every month. Margaret herself had contributed a recipe for a fruit cake using dried fruit soaked in tea – everyone had loved it and there had been several requests for the recipe.

Within an hour the tea room was buzzing, most of the tables were taken, many with people who were visiting the area. Several asked Ellie which were the best places to visit. She usually named a few she'd visited herself such as the Corinium Museum and the Arboretum. She always suggested they visit a few of the shops in the older buildings with their maze of rooms and uneven floors as this was interesting for the visitors and usually good business for the local stores. If the weather was good she'd also recommend taking a walk in the Abbey Grounds to see a little of the town's Roman history.

As was usual in the morning Pat made up a selection of sandwiches and, if they were needed, baked some cakes before giving Ellie a hand with serving the customers. Ellie could already smell the delicious aroma of warm cakes. As she headed back towards the kitchen with an order for sandwiches another customer walked through the door, a man wearing a navy suit, white shirt and one of those picture ties that were using bought by children for their father – this one was covered with rabbits. He looked like he was popping in during a break from work. Occasionally people walked in wanting a coffee to go, this was one of the things she had decided not to offer. She wanted people to take the time to enjoy their tea, or coffee, and she liked to have a little time, even if only a few minutes, to chat with her customers.

Ellie looked at the man and smiled. "Can I help?" she said. "Would you like a table?"

"No, thanks," he said. "I wanted to order a birthday cake, your sign in the window says you make any design to order."

"We do," Ellie said looking around the busy room, she always wanted to make all of her customers feel welcome but now was not a great time to discuss cake designs.

"Take a seat," Ellie said gesturing to an empty table. "I'll just be a minute."

She asked Pat to take over in the tea room and grabbed her file of photos she'd taken of the cakes she'd made and a few ideas for themes.

"I'm Ellie, I may need to keep popping up to serve, unless you'd prefer to come back later when it's a bit quieter," said Ellie as she sat opposite him.

"I'm Michael," said the man. "I realise you're busy but I'd like to order now if that's possible. I looking to buy a cake for a birthday party and a want something a bit special, well very special actually."

"I make to order so I can do pretty much any theme you want, when's the party?" asked Ellie.

"This weekend," said Michael.

Ellie looked up in surprise. "This weekend, as in five days away? You're cutting it fine. I can certainly do something but I usually work to a three week turnaround to allow enough time to plan the design and create the decorations," she said.

"Sorry," Michael said, "it was a bit of a last minute decision. Grace has been unwell for quite a while and has been in and out of hospital for the last few months. She's well enough for a party now, her birthday was actually six weeks ago but she was in hospital. I wanted something really special, something that would do a bit more than make her smile.

"Of course I'll do my best," Ellie said, smiling. "How old is Grace?"

"Nine," Michael replied.

Ellie smiled at him. "Let's have a look at some examples and see if there's anything you like," she said.

She opened the file and showed Michael some of the photos of the cakes she'd made in the past.

"This one was for a little boy, he was mad about spiders

so I made this cake like a giant spider on a web. I had to make the spider look friendly as I didn't want to scare the other children," she said. "I'm guessing not what you want for a little girl."

She flicked through to another that was made up of individual cupcakes each decorated slightly differently and with a name iced onto each. "This one was for a wedding anniversary, they wanted it to show how important each one of their friends and family were to them," she said. "These probably aren't what you are looking for but there are some themes here around Halloween, football, and horse-riding."

She continued to turn the pages but even though Michael made positive comments his face didn't seem to light up to any of them. Ellie closed the file.

"Perhaps the cupcake idea would be nice," he said.

Ellie looked at him and smiled. "I can design something specifically for Grace, perhaps a favourite hobby, but we'll have to be quick as I'll need to start tonight. What does Grace like most of all?" Ellie asked.

Michael looked thoughtful for a moment. "She likes fairies, could you do something that includes them. I'm sorry, I'm not great when it comes to imagination," he said.

"I'll give it some thought tonight, can you come back tomorrow morning and I'll run some ideas by you," Ellie said. "In the meantime I'll need to get on with baking the cake, how many people is it for and what type of cake do you want – sponge, fruit, chocolate?"

"Wow, all these choices," Michael said laughing. "There'll be about twelve children and a quite a few family so maybe enough for thirty. Sponge I guess, could it be purple, it's her favourite colour?"

"Purple sponge it is," Ellie said as she stood up. "Pop in tomorrow before ten, I'm sure I can come up with something she'll like."

Ellie watched Michael leave, she had no idea who Grace was, however, clearly this birthday party was important and Michael wanted it to be perfect. All she had to do was deliver a cake in just four and a half days.

As Ellie cleared a few tables Jessica walked into the tea room.

"Come to help?" asked Ellie.

Jessica laughed. "I know you're busy so I've arranged to see some old friends. I'll be back this evening and then we can talk properly. Maybe talk about the future - yours and mine," she said.

Ellie watched as she left. She felt the urge to go after her and tell her they could talk now. With that two more customers came in. She couldn't leave Pat on her own so it would have to wait.

4

Jessica hadn't returned by the time Ellie closed the tea room, she wasn't too surprised as Jessica had said she'd be back later that evening. Although something was obviously troubling her she didn't seem too distressed. Whatever it was she hoped she'd share it soon. She popped a chicken casserole in the oven, if Jessica wasn't hungry she could warm it up another day.

Now seemed a good time to start on the cake for Michael, if she was going to get it finished she needed to get a move on. Ellie did most of her baking in the tea room kitchen, there were some practical reasons such as two good ovens and a pantry full of ingredients however the main reason she like being downstairs was because she could look through the window and watch the evening walkers and night-time revellers walking past. There was a predictability about people at different times of the night, early evening a few people were walking dogs or popping to get milk, a little later people were dressed up to meet friends and enjoy a meal or drink, occasionally there might be couples walking together, and later everyone made their way back home – often rather noisily. This gave her a sense of time moving on rather than standing still as it had done when she'd first had the news that James had been killed. In the early years she could put the twins to bed and come down here, she always took the baby monitor with her, even when they got older, just to be sure they were safe.

Before she'd baked she'd had this vast stretch of time, night after night, to think of the past and the injustice of it all. Her grief had started to crush her. A chance conversation with a customer led her to making first one, and then many, celebration cakes. With her waking hours filled she had been able to start to rebuild a life for her and the twins.

Ellie took the scales from the shelf, weighed out the flour and sieved it into the mixing bowl. She then added the sugar, butter and eggs. Finally, she combined the ingredients in her mixer setting it at a slow speed to start before turning it up to get a nice fluffy texture. The large red mixer had been a present to herself, she'd seen it in a cook shop in the town and bought it on impulse. It always made her smile when she used it, it made her feel like a proper cook.

Once the mixture had a light and fluffy look she divided it between two bowls and added some pink colouring to one bowl and purple to the other. She then carefully folded the two mixtures together to get a marbled effect.

Ellie divided the mixture between three tins, two would make up a tiered cake and the last would be used to cut out some additional shapes if needed. She kept a little mixture back to make some cupcakes for Michael to try tomorrow.

As she put the cakes into the oven and set the timer Jessica walked into the kitchen.

"Can I help?" Jessica asked.

"Since when have you been interested in baking?" Ellie said laughing.

"Well, I could learn," Jessica replied.

"I've pretty much finished tonight but you can help tidy up," Ellie said.

"Washing up, that brings back memories," Jessica said collecting the bowls from the worktop.

"Don't worry, I've invested in a dishwasher, the mixer will have to be washed by hand though," Ellie said as she filled the sink with warm water.

Jessica sat down on a stool. "You know I've always loved this place, it holds so many memories, good memories," she said.

Ellie smiled at her, she was about to ask her why she was here when there was a knock on the door.

Ellie looked across the tea room and could see a familiar face pressed against the door. It was Edward, Jessica's husband.

"Hi," she said after she'd unlocked the door and let Edward in.

Edward rushed across the room. "Jessica, what's the matter?" he said. "I got your text and came as soon as I could, is everything alright?"

"Oh Jessica," Ellie said. "I thought you were going to ring him."

"I was," she replied looking annoyed, "tonight."

Ellie went back to the kitchen to clear up and put the cakes on a cooling tray but she couldn't help but overhear their conversation.

"I just want some time on my own," Jessica said. "I had to get away."

"Are you feeling okay?" Edward asked with genuine concern in his voice.

"Yes, I'm fine, in fact I've never felt better," Jessica said.

"I guess a rest would be good for you at the moment," he said.

"I don't need a rest, I need a normal life," Jessica said.

"I get the feeling something's wrong but I've no idea what it is, tell me and then we can sort it out," Edward said.

Ellie watched Jessica take a deep breath, she looked as if she was about to scream at Edward or at least start shouting at him. Maybe now was a good time to intervene, she walked into the tea room and looked at Edward.

"I was just about to dish up supper," she said. "Would you like to stay?"

"Edward has a long journey back," Jessica answered, "and the M4 can be a nightmare in the evening."

"A spot of food will do you good then," Ellie said.

Jessica looked at Edward. "You didn't need to drive down here, you could have just telephoned me," she said. Her voice had lost some of its edge.

"I tried but you didn't answer, and I just wanted to make sure you were alright, your text said you'd come here and you didn't know how long you'd be staying," Edward said. "I thought something terrible had happened. How long are you staying?"

"Not sure, I've booked a week off work," Jessica

answered.

"That'll give me time to finish the nursery," Edward said smiling.

"You don't need to finish the nursery, there's plenty of time to do that," Jessica said, her voice rising again.

"I know but we want to be ready," Edward said. "The next few months will fly by."

"Look just go back home," Jessica said.

Edward looked hurt. "I know you're tired at the moment but I am trying you know. This is all new to me as well," he said.

"Maybe, but it's not going to change your life is it?" Jessica said.

"Of course it is, and I'm glad." Edward said. "I can't wait for the days out at football matches or ballet classes and, of course, another brother or sister."

"Stop, okay, just stop. I'm going to bed, I'm too tired for this right now," Jessica said. She walked out of the tea room into the hall.

Edward looked at Ellie. "I guess she's not feeling great right now but I don't know what else to do," he said.

Ellie noticed his eyes were brimming with tears. "I don't know what's wrong but I'll try and have a talk with her," Ellie said. "Do you want something to eat before you go?"

"No thanks, I'd better get back else I'll only make things worse," Edward replied.

"Well drive safely and stay in touch," Ellie said. She put her hand on Edward's shoulder. "I'm sure it'll be fine. She just needs some time."

After Edward had gone Jessica came back into the tea room and sat at one of the tables. She pulled a corner of the tablecloth into her hand and started to twist it.

"What was that all about?" Ellie asked. "It did seem like you were being a little unfair, unless there's something you're not telling me."

"You wouldn't understand," Jessica said.

"Try me," Ellie said trying to keep her voice as gentle as

she could.

"I'm tired Mum. Can we talk about it tomorrow?" Jessica said. She dropped the corner of the tablecloth and stood up. "I really am going to bed now."

5

Michael knocked on the door at nine-thirty. Ellie made a pot of tea and laid a tray for two. This tea was grown in Cornwall, she'd only discovered it recently and it had quickly become a bestseller.

"Here's a sample of the cake," she said. She gave him a lilac and pink coloured cupcake covered in green icing with little silver stars on top.

Michael bit into it. "Mmm, this is delicious," he said. "Grace will love it."

"I've had some thoughts about the cake," Ellie said. "What do you think about a woodland scene with fairies having a party around a fire? I could include a tree trunk with a hollow, some little strings of lights and some logs for the fairies to sit on."

"That sounds fantastic," he said. "Is that possible by the weekend?"

"I'll do my best, one way or another you'll have a cake by Saturday morning," Ellie replied. "Can I ask about Grace, is she your daughter?"

"No, she's my niece," he replied, "I told my sister I'd organise this party, she's got enough to deal with at the moment and, to be honest, I wanted to do something to help. I've felt a bit useless during the past few months."

Ellie watched as Michael looked down at his teacup, she could see the look of concern and worry in the lines on his face. She didn't want to pry any further, Michael would tell her more if he wanted to.

"Ring me on Saturday morning before you come to collect," Ellie said. She handed him a business card.

"Will do," he said as he got up to leave. "And thank you, you're going to make a little girl very happy."

Ellie turned to clear the table and heard the bell jingle as Michael left.

"Hi Mum," a voice said.

"Marie," Ellie said with surprise. "I don't see either of you for months and then you both visit out of the blue."

"What do you mean?" Marie said looking a little confused, "I had this sudden urge to come and visit. I've just finished a contract and had a little time to kill so I jumped in the car and here I am."

"Jessica's here," Ellie said.

"Is she alright?" Marie said sounding concerned.

"She's fine, well maybe not totally fine. I'll let her explain," Ellie said realising she still didn't have a clue what was wrong with Jessica.

"Sounds like we're the proverbial bad pennies," Marie said laughing.

"No, I'm just surprised to see you both, a nice surprise though," Ellie said as she cleared away the tea tray.

"Mum, is it okay if I stay a few days? Like I said I'm between contracts so it seemed like a good time to take a break," Marie said heading towards the hall door.

"You, take a break, that's a novelty. I'm not sure you've stopped since uni," Ellie said.

"I know, I know. But with Jessica getting married and having a baby I've just been thinking that maybe I need to stay in touch a bit more," Marie said.

"Before you go up I've got something to tell you." Jessica said.

"Sounds ominous," said Marie. "Do you have a new man in your life?" she asked laughing as she pushed open the door to the hall.

"No, I'm selling the tea room," Ellie replied quietly.

"Selling or thinking of selling?" Marie asked letting go of the door.

"Selling. The photographer came round yesterday and the brochure will be ready any day soon so keep your room tidy in case I get any viewings," Ellie said.

"But Mum, are you sure you've thought this through, this place is you, you can't give it to someone else," Marie said looking directly at her mother.

"I'm not giving it to anyone, I'm selling it. And maybe it was me but things change," Ellie said.

"What could possibly change?" Marie asked.

"You may not have noticed but I've been living here on my own for most of the last five years, so now is a good time to do something else," Ellie said. She really didn't think her daughters would be that bothered about the sale.

"Marie," Jessica screeched as she walked into the tea room. "What are you doing here?"

"I could ask the same of you," Marie said.

"Are you staying?" Jessica asked.

"Yes, for a while," Marie replied.

"Great, I need someone to have some fun with, it'll be just like old times," Jessica said hugging her sister.

Ellie looked at them both and smiled. "I'll make a pot of tea," she said.

6

Ellie didn't see much of the girls for the rest of the day, she was busy in the tea room and they were upstairs catching up. They did pop down once to see what sandwiches and cakes they could take for their lunch – at least some things never changed.

When the last customer had left Ellie turned over the closed sign, at last she had some time to catch up with her twins, she still had no idea why either of them had turned up out of the blue. She was always really pleased to see them but this was uncharacteristic, usually they planned their visits weeks ahead and rarely stopped overnight.

As Ellie straightened the chairs Jessica poked her head around the door.

"Bye Mum, we're off, there's a band playing locally so we're meeting up with some old friends. Don't worry about tea, we're eating out," said Jessica.

"Oh, okay," Ellie said. "I was hoping we could have a chat."

"We can," said Jessica as she walked into the tea room and gave her mother a hug. "Tomorrow."

Marie followed behind her. "We haven't had time together in ages, we'd almost forgotten how much fun we used to have," Marie said. "You don't mind do you?"

They weren't identical, in looks anyway, but sometimes they seemed so alike. They now led very different lives – Marie had her career and Jessica was married and expecting a baby. And yet when they were together they seemed more than similar - laughing at the same jokes, having the same opinion, even enjoying the same music. They definitely had a connection beyond being sisters. They always seemed to know when the other needed support, like today when Marie turned up shortly after Jessica.

"Of course not," Ellie said smiling. "You two enjoy yourself, perhaps we can have breakfast together tomorrow."

"That would be great," Jessica said. "We'll even cook so you can have a lie in."

"Well that'll be a first, have a great time," Ellie said as she watched them leave.

At least she'd have some time to get on with the cake this evening. A quick shower and something to eat and then she'd start work. She went upstairs and into the sitting room. She sighed. Make-up, a hairdryer, a mirror and various brushes were strewn across the coffee table. Ellie picked everything up and carried it all into the girls' bedrooms. Brings back memories, she thought. Jessica's bedroom was a real mess, clothes were strewn across the bed, floor, chair, everywhere except in the wardrobe. Even when she lived at home she generally wasn't this untidy, she hadn't even made her bed. Marie's bedroom wasn't much better, the only reason the bed was made was because she hadn't slept in in yet. Ellie shut the bedroom doors, at least there were no viewings tomorrow.

After she had eaten the remainder of last night's casserole Ellie went back down to the kitchen and took the cakes off the shelf. When she had baked them she didn't have a clear idea of what she was going to create, now she realised she would need both of the two smaller cakes to make her tree trunk. She placed one small cake on top of the other and then placed these on top of the larger square cake. The tree trunk was much too big, she'd have quite a lot of trimming and shaping to do. Ellie took great care in cutting the cakes to size and then removing a considerable amount from the centre to create the hollow. She put them back on the large cake, much better, now there was plenty of room to build up a scene. It would all be iced and decorated but she needed to get the structure right first. She looked at the offcuts of cake. Enough to create two logs for the fairies to sit on. She put the remainder in a tub – just in case. Tomorrow she could start icing and creating the flowers, toadstools and some small woodland animals.

Once she had finished with the cake Ellie flicked through her catalogue of decorations. She found some traditional looking fairies, quite grown up ones, and turned on her iPad to order them, she selected next day delivery but assumed they'd actually arrive the day after. Next, she browsed her favourite website of dolls house furniture and accessories and found some battery operated miniature strings of lights and a wood effect fire she could use as the basis for a camp fire. She particularly liked this site as she often found really nice miniature items she could use on her cakes. As always she'd give advice on the items used to ensure everyone knew they were not edible and not toys.

It was after eleven when she finished. She was making a mug of hot chocolate when she heard the girls come back.

"Did you have a good time?" Ellie asked. Not that she needed to ask judging by the noise they made as they came up the stairs.

"Yes, it was great, it's good to be back," Jessica said.

"I'd forgotten how much I love this place," Marie said.

"Well I remember a time when you both couldn't wait to get away, what was it you used to say – you wanted the big city, lots of lights and plenty of parties," Ellie said.

She remembered when they had first gone away to university, Jessica to Bristol and Marie to Manchester. It was at Bristol that Jessica had met Edward, when they'd graduated they'd both got jobs in the city, bought a house, got married, very much a fairy tale wedding, and were now having their first baby.

Marie, on the other hand, had been totally focussed on having a career. She'd had the occasional boyfriend but nothing serious. She'd moved to London and worked for one of the big advertising agencies, she'd worked day and night to ensure she got the promotions she wanted. She'd managed to buy a small apartment fairly close to the centre, no mean feat on her own and with London prices. She was living her life exactly as she'd planned it.

Neither Jessica nor Marie had shown any interest in staying in the small Cotswold town, in fact they'd probably used the word boring on more than one occasion.

"Yeah we know, but that was when we were younger," Marie said looking at Jessica.

"It wasn't that many years ago," Ellie said, "you're not exactly elderly."

"Maybe we've just got it out of our system," Jessica said. She looked at Marie and winked.

"Maybe. Well I don't know about you two but I've got to get up tomorrow so I'm off to bed," Ellie said yawning.

As she wandered into her bedroom she could hear her daughters talking about their evening and the friends they'd met up with. It sounded like they'd had a really good time and were enjoying being back here. Perhaps they'd visit more often when she moved.

7

The next morning Ellie woke up to the sound of her alarm. Alarm was a good word as she never slept this late, she only ever set it as a bit of security, just in case. Well this was one of those just in case mornings – she desperately wanted to crawl under her duvet and go back to sleep but instead she got up and headed for the bathroom. There was no smell of cooking bacon or fresh coffee so she guessed there wasn't the promised cooked breakfast waiting for her. As she passed the girls' bedrooms she could see they were not getting up anytime soon, that early morning chat would have to wait.

Half an hour later she opened the tea room door to let Pat in.

"Late night?" Pat enquired.

"Getting this cake done," Ellie said struggling to suppress a yawn.

"You really should stick to your guns and say no to these short notice ones, people should plan ahead," Pat said.

"I know, but this is different," Ellie said. "Somehow it really did seem important."

"I thought you'd have help this morning, what with having the girls back," Pat said as she put on her apron.

"I was hoping that too but they did have a late night, flat out both of them," Ellie said indicating upstairs.

"Well we'd better get a move on if we're going to open on time," Pat said as she headed for the kitchen.

Ellie rushed around changing tablecloths, checking salt and pepper pots and filling the sugar bowls with the little brown and white cubes she liked to use. The water hadn't heated by the time the first customer arrived, if they wanted tea she'd have to boil the kettle.

By lunchtime the place was full and people were waiting for tables. When this happened she operated a simple number system, she gave the waiting customer a numbered ticket and then called the numbers as a table became clear, it seemed more civilised than having people dash towards a table as soon as someone looked like they were reaching for their coat.

As she grabbed a tray of tea and spoke to a customer wanting to pay Jessica and Marie pop their heads through the door.

"We're off now," Jessica said. "We're going into Bath to do a spot of shopping, it's great being able to spend so much time together."

Ellie took a deep breath and smiled at them. "Have a nice time," she said. They didn't even seem to notice that she was run off her feet and could do with a little help. She thought it was great they were enjoying themselves and this probably seemed like a bit of a holiday for them but she couldn't help but worry about what their next move might be.

8

Once they had closed the tea room Ellie decided to grab a few sandwiches and get on with the cake. She mixed up a big batch of icing and divided it into smaller bowls to add colouring. A mid-green for the forest floor, brown might have been more realistic but with the tree trunk being brown she wanted some contrast. A dark brown for the tree trunk and logs and a dark green to create the effect of moss. She used a little icing to fix the layers of cake in place and then covered it all with the different coloured icing. Ellie used a knife to create a rough texture for the forest floor and a bark effect on the trunk. She decorated the two logs on a board and then carefully placed them on the cake. Finally, she added touches of dark green. Already the cake was starting to come alive. She covered it and placed it back on the shelf. One more night to complete it, there was still a lot to do but at least it was now looking achievable.

The girls hadn't yet arrived home from their shopping trip, Ellie decided to send them a text to let them know she was having an early night and would catch up with them in the morning. With that she turned off the lights and headed upstairs.

9

Ellie woke to the sun streaming through the window, this weather really was fantastic for the time of year and it was certainly bringing in plenty of customers, the seasonal staff weren't starting till next week but she was going to need some help today. She put the kettle on, went back into the hall and called Marie and Jessica.

"Come on you two, you can help me today, I'm expecting to be busy," Ellie said as she opened their bedroom doors.

There was no sound from Marie however Jessica mumbled, "okay, we'll pop down when we're up and dressed." With that she pulled the duvet over her head.

"No, you'll get up now and be downstairs before opening," Ellie said.

She went into Marie's room and opened the curtains.

"Oh Mum," said Marie covering her eyes. "I need more sleep."

"So do I but we've got a tea room to open so get up and be downstairs in half an hour," Ellie said.

"I can't be ready in that time," Marie protested.

"Yes, you can. Just get showered and tie your hair back. You can have a coffee and something to eat downstairs," Ellie said. "And make your beds," she shouted to them both as she went back into the kitchen.

Ellie made herself a coffee, went downstairs and started to prepare for opening. She did her usual round of putting on new cloths and turning on the hot water. Forty minutes later the twins walked into the tea room.

"It's not even opening time yet, surely we could have had an extra hour in bed," Marie said yawning. "What do you want us to do? We thought Jessica could greet and seat and I could take orders."

"Firstly, we need to get ready for opening, so could you both refill all the salt and pepper pots and check the cutlery.

I'll do the flowers." Ellie said.

"Don't you do all this the night before?" Jessica asked clearly surprised that they had to do anything more than unlock the door and display the open sign.

"I clean up the night before, that takes long enough," Ellie said. "Everything else is done in the morning. And secondly once the customers arrive could one of you clear the tables as people leave and the other do the washing up."

"Don't you have staff to wash up?" Marie asked.

"There's just the two of us this time of year and Pat needs to do the food whilst I take orders and prepare the bills. We share making teas and coffees. If we get a quiet time you're welcome to learn the ropes. And Jessica make sure you take breaks and sit down when you need to but tell me or Pat," Ellie said. The girls had been away for some time but she had expected they might remember a little of how much work went into running the tea room.

"Okay, Mum," Marie said. "Come on Jessica, let's get started."

"I've got a viewing booked in today so I'll need to leave you to it for a while, Pat will be in charge whilst I'm out," Ellie said looking away but not fast enough to miss seeing their look of disapproval.

Ellie watched them fill the salt and pepper pots whilst she put fresh flowers into the vases. She could hear them mumbling to each other and caught the odd word – something about this being some holiday. As Ellie put the last vase on the table Pat arrived.

"Morning girls," Pat said looking at Ellie with surprise.

"Morning," both girls replied with little enthusiasm in their voices.

"They're helping all day," Ellie said to Pat.

With that the first customer arrived. Ellie took their order and made up a pot of tea whilst Pat made up the sandwiches. A few moments later six people walked in.

"Jessica could you let Pat know we have a large table and then stay in the kitchen to tidy and wash up," Ellie said. "And

Marie could you be ready to carry the teas and cakes to the tables."

"How come Marie gets the best job," Jessica said pulling a face.

"You can swap over in an hour," Ellie said, this seemed very much like working with a couple of teenagers except the teenagers she usually worked with didn't act like spoilt kids.

By midday the tea room was buzzing with most of the tables taken and a couple waiting to be seated.

"Come on Marie," Ellie said. "You need to get these tables cleared, we've people waiting."

"I'm doing the best I can," Marie said, "When's lunch break?"

"This is a tea room, you get a lunch break after lunch," Ellie said.

"This is slave labour," Marie said.

"This is reality, if you need a drink or are hungry ask Jessica to come out here so you can take ten minutes in the backroom. Only ten minutes though as we're about to hit our busy time," Ellie said.

"Busy time, how much busier can it get?" Marie said as she cleared another table.

****

At two o'clock the first potential buyers arrived to view the tea room, the estate agent had already told her the young couple were looking to move into the area and were particularly looking for a business to run together.

"Come on in, I'm Ellie," Ellie said. "Have you come far?"

"Not too far, Gloucester," the lady said. "I'm Sam and this is Chris." She held out her hand.

"I'll give you the tour, please ask me anything as we go," Ellie said leading the way to the kitchen.

"What's happened here?" Ellie said as she looked around the kitchen to see most surfaces covered with dirty dishes.

"And where's Jessica?"

"Sorry," said Pat looking embarrassed, "Jessica went for a break a while ago, I'll go and find her when I've finished this order."

Ellie felt a flush on cheeks, her kitchen never looked like this, even when they were busy.

Ellie looked at the young couple. "We've had a surge of customers the last few days, the weather's brought them out I think, unfortunately the seasonal staff don't start until next week and it appears the unpaid help has gone AWOL," she said.

Sam and Chris both laughed, they didn't seem to be put off by the kitchen, and hopefully they could see beyond the dirty dishes.

Ellie took the couple upstairs, luckily the girls had left it reasonably tidy.

"These are my daughters' rooms," she said as she opened both doors. "I would say typical teenagers but they're a bit older than that."

At least the beds were made, not exactly the clean and tidy look she'd hoped for but they looked lived in rather than a total mess.

"This is just the kind of place we're looking for. We've seen a few places and some just looked staged," Chris said, "almost as if no-one really lives there."

Ellie smiled. "I know what you mean," she said.

"If it's okay we'd like to come back with my parents," Sam said. "They're helping us buy a place so we'd like their opinion."

"Of course," Ellie said. "Come on downstairs and I'll make you a pot of tea."

When they went back into the tea room things seemed a bit calmer, there were still a lot of customers however the empty tables were cleared and no one seemed to be waiting. She'd make up a proper afternoon tea for Sam and Chris, that should give them a chance to get a feel for the place and hopefully give her a chance to show them that they didn't live and work in permanent chaos.

10

"Tea's ready," Ellie called out to her daughters.

Jessica and Marie walked into the kitchen as Ellie took the macaroni cheese out of the oven and placed it on the kitchen table alongside a bowl of salad tossed in her homemade dressing.

Ellie smiled. "This used to be the one time of day we could always spend together," she said.

"I did enjoy just sitting here and chatting," Jessica said.

"Are you going out tonight?" Ellie asked her daughters.

"No," they both said together. They looked at each other. "Too tired."

Marie looked at Ellie. "Look mum, we've been talking, we really don't think you should sell the tea room, we both love this place. We know you've worked hard and deserve to take more of a break so we thought I could do a business plan that will help you improve your profits, then you can hire more staff," Marie said looking quite serious.

Ellie took a deep breath. "As thoughtful as that is it is time for a change. If I kept the place on I wouldn't be able to let go. You know I've loved this place but I'm ready for something new. Let me show you the cottage, I've got the details here," she said.

Ellie took the brochure from the kitchen drawer, she smiled as she looked at the photograph on the front.

"Take a look," she said handing the details to Marie, "there are some lovely photos of the place, I'm sure you can see why I fell in love with it."

Marie glanced at the photo on the front and handed the details to Jessica. "Mum, this place is tiny, where are we going to stay?" she asked.

"It's got a spare room, and I can put a sofa bed in the sitting room if you are both down together. There's also an attic room, I'd need to do it up but that would be an extra room," Ellie said smiling at Jessica, "for the grandchildren."

"Don't you think you're being a little selfish selling the family home without talking to us first?" Marie said. "We could help you find a more suitable house."

"I think it's time to be a little selfish," said Ellie.

"I know," Jessica said with enthusiasm. "I could come back and help you."

"But what about Edward?" Ellie asked.

"I don't know, I'm not sure I want to go back," Jessica said quietly.

"Now you of all people should know how hard it is to bring up a child on your own," Ellie said.

"But I wouldn't be on my own," Jessica said looking down. "I'd have you."

"You know you're always welcome here but you also know how much a father is needed," Ellie said.

"I wished I'd known Dad," Jessica said with tears in her eyes. "I can't even say I have any memories. There's the odd time when something pops into my head and there's definitely a man in the picture but I can't see him, no details, not even the colour of his hair."

"You've got the photos," Ellie said.

"But I can't superimpose them onto my memories," Jessica said. The tears had started to fall down her cheeks.

"You were very young, only two when he died." Ellie said. She looked at her daughters and smiled. "Do you know he was over the moon when I was pregnant, when I told him we were having twins I remember him saying, 'excellent, two for the price of one.' When you were born he absolutely adored you both, I think he was secretly pleased you had different coloured hair though, he was really worried he wouldn't be able to tell you apart."

Jessica looked up. "Tell me more about him," she said.

"He would get up in the night if you cried and sing you back to sleep. Sometimes he'd get up even if you were settled and look at you both with such pride. You were fourteen months old when we took you on your first holiday. He held you by the edge of the sea and dangled your feet in the water."

Ellie said. "I remember, Jessica, how you insisted on walking and then screamed as a wave came and covered your knees. Your father scooped you up and told the wave off just to make you laugh. You copied him Marie, you pointed your finger at the sea and made a very cross face," Ellie said laughing. "He would have been so proud of you both, he would have loved your graduations, the wedding and now the birth of his first grandchild."

Marie smiled at her mother. She had her eyes half closed as if trying to recreate the scenes in her mind. "So why didn't you marry again, or at least have someone else in your life? It's been a long time since Dad died, I'm sure he wouldn't have minded," she said.

"No, he wouldn't have minded," Ellie said. "For the first year or two I didn't really come to terms with the fact he wasn't coming back – ever." Ellie closed her eyes. "As you know I received a visit from two police officers and they told me there'd been an accident at his workplace, an explosion and fire. Three people died that day. Good job I had you both else I don't think I'd have got out of bed ever again. Having two year old twins was enough to fill more than the twenty-four hours I had each day. After the funeral and inquest I decided to move away and came here to Cirencester. At that point I had two demanding twins and a business to run so that didn't leave much time, or rather any time, for anything else. And I wouldn't have had it any other way." She opened her eyes and brushed away the tears that had started to form.

"So how come you're selling if you've invested so much into this place, if it means so much to you?" Jessica asked.

Ellie looked at her daughters and reached across to touch their hands. "I guess I've finally reached a point where I don't need it anymore," she said softly.

Ellie picked up a spoon and served up tea. "After we've eaten I have to finish the cake," she said. "Why don't you both get an early night? I could really do with your help tomorrow, after that perhaps we can have a day out together."

11

Ellie went back downstairs to the kitchen. She'd left the girls watching a film together, something they hadn't done since they'd finished university and gone their separate ways. She knew they stayed in touch and she often heard about the epic phone calls but there didn't seem to be much time for them to actually spend time relaxing together. Perhaps after these last few days they might try and meet up more often.

Ellie took the cake off the shelf, this was it, the last evening to turn the cake into something that would put a smile on Grace's face, and perhaps her mum's too. She took the battery operated fire, placed it on the cake and surrounded it with the logs she'd created. When she turned on the little light the fire looked quite realistic.

She pulled a stool up to the central table, sat down and began to mould toadstools and flowers. Once they were ready she painted them with food colouring. Ellie really enjoyed painting her creations rather than colouring the icing beforehand, the tiny variations meant that each decoration was unique. Whilst they dried Ellie placed the fairies on the cake and draped the strings of lights around the scene. Finally, she added the tiny flowers and toadstools.

Ellie looked at the scene and smiled, it really did look magical. As she stood up Jessica and Marie walked into the kitchen.

"We're sorry Mum," said Jessica, "for going on about you selling the tea room. It was just such a surprise."

Ellie walked across to her daughters and gave them both a hug. "I should have told you sooner, but I really didn't think you'd be that interested," she said.

"We'll help you finish up," said Marie, "it'll be just like the old times."

"Not the old times as I remember them," Ellie said laughing. "Perhaps we can start some new old times and you two can help with the washing up."

"I get to lick the spoon," said Jessica as she reached across the worktop to grab the bowl with the remains of the icing.

Marie laughed and also reached for the bowl.

Everything seemed to be in slow motion. The girls reached for the bowl, it slid across the table, knocked the cake stand and the cake slid off the table onto the floor. As it hit the floor it split and crumbled.

Ellie looked in disbelief, she couldn't speak, she felt hot tears trickle down her face. She had put her heart and soul into this cake, she'd wanted it to be as near perfect as possible, and now it was just a pile of crumbs. Ellie put her head in her hands and sobbed.

"Oh, Mum," said Marie. "We're so sorry."

Ellie looked up at the distraught look in their faces. This was just an accident after all, no-one had meant for this to happen but knowing this didn't help, she couldn't control her tears as they continued to drip onto the cake on the floor.

"Perhaps you could make another," said Jessica. "It would only take a couple of hours to put together a sponge and a bit of icing, I'm sure there are some candles around here somewhere.

Ellie looked at Jessica. "I don't want to put a bit of icing on a cake with a few candles," she said trying to keep her voice steady. "Not only do I never do that, this cake was meant to be special, for a little girl who's been through so much."

"Do you know her?" Marie asked.

"No, but I know about her and by making this cake I could have made a little difference to her life," Ellie said as she started to scoop up the cake from the floor.

Marie looked up. "It was an accident," she said.

"I know, I know," Ellie said softly.

Jessica walked over to the cupboard and took out the flour and sugar. "Come on," she said. "We can't put that one back together but we can make another." She sounded unusually assertive.

"He's collecting it in the morning," Ellie said.

"Well we'd better get a move on then," Jessica said taking the scales down from the shelf.

"Marie, you clean up the floor, we don't want any more mishaps, I'll turn on the ovens and Mum, you can do the magic by mixing it all together," Jessica said sounding quite bright.

"But," said Ellie.

"No buts, if we don't start we won't finish," said Jessica firmly.

Ellie looked at Jessica, she'd never looked so confident, so in control. Well she'd better do as she was told and start mixing.

Three hours later the cake was cooked, cooled, and cut ready to start the build. Ellie instructed Jessica and Marie on how to mix the icing and which colours to add. She started to build the tree with its hollow and cover the cake with green and brown icing. By one o'clock they had the basis of a woodland scene. Under Ellie's instruction they made branches, a log fire, toadstools, and tiny flowers. As she carefully placed each handmade object onto the scene the cake started to look magical. Together they added the fairies and little strings of battery operated lights that twinkled through the scene. At four o'clock the cake was finished. They carefully covered it and gave it a final look before turning out the kitchen lights.

Jessica laughed and turned to Marie. "When I said I fancied an all-nighter this wasn't what I had in mind," she said.

"Thank you," Ellie said hugging her two daughters.

"No Mum, thank you," said Jessica.

"Yes," said Marie. "Thank you, for everything. And even though I'll miss this place you're right, it is time for you to sell."

Ellie felt more tears run down her face. This time she let them fall.

12

Michael arrived at nine-thirty.

"Wow," he said when Ellie brought out the cake. "I can't believe you did this in less than a week, I have to admit that with the timescale I'd given you I was expecting a bit of icing and some candles."

Ellie laughed. "As if," she said.

"Grace will love it, I can't thank you enough," Michael said taking the cake box from her.

Ellie smiled and suppressed a yawn. "It was my pleasure, or should I say our pleasure," she said, thinking of the daughters she'd left in bed. "Give Grace my love and I hope she enjoys her party."

Michael paused. "Could I take you out for a drink, perhaps tomorrow lunchtime, as a way of saying thank-you," he said.

"You've already thanked me, and it really was a pleasure even if a little challenging," Ellie said.

"Please, I would very much like to," Michael said a little hesitantly.

Ellie looked at him, he did seem nice enough, she didn't know him at all but perhaps now was the time to take a small risk, meeting at a local pub couldn't hurt.

"Okay, I'd like that," she said.

"Shall I pick you up, I know a lovely place a few miles from here," he said smiling.

"I'd rather stay in town if that's alright, there's a great place just up the road. I've got my daughters visiting so I don't want to be away too long," Ellie said.

"Up the road it is then, if I don't have to drive I can join you with a drink," Michael said.

Michael picked up the cake and left just as Marie walked into the tea room wearing her dressing gown.

"I overheard that," Marie said grinning. "I know we said you should meet someone but we didn't mean arrange a date with the first stranger you see."

"He's not a complete stranger," Ellie said. "Anyway I'm not sure I want to go out with any of the men I actually know especially as most of them are married."

"Shall we come with you just in case?" Marie said.

"I don't think so," Ellie said. "I'm a grown woman, I'll be fine."

Ellie smiled remembering the times she'd been tempted to follow her daughters on their dates – just in case. She didn't actually do it, instead she just stayed awake until they came home and then pretended she'd been asleep for ages. How times had changed, she certainly hadn't expected this role reversal.

13

Ellie turned the sign on the tea room door to open. Today was going to be another hot one which meant busy. As she walked back to the kitchen the bell jingled.

"Hi Ellie," Edward called. "Is it okay to come in?"

"Of course," Ellie said. "Jessica's upstairs." Whatever the problem was between Jessica and Edward she hoped they could work it out.

"If it's alright with Jessica could I stay?" Edward asked as he headed towards the hall door. "I'm not sure what her plans are but I'd like to spend some time with her."

"Sure," Ellie said. "It'd be good if you two can sort things out."

Edward looked at her. "I'm not sure there's much to sort out. She's been a bit tired and techy but hopefully the rest has done her good," he said.

"Edward, I do think you should talk to her, see what's on her mind," Ellie said. "I don't know what's wrong but clearly something's troubling her."

Edward had a look of concern on his face. "I'll do that," he said.

Ellie followed him up the stairs and into the kitchen, she needed a quick caffeine fix before starting work.

Surprisingly Marie and Jessica were already up and, even more surprisingly they were washing up their breakfast bowls.

"Hi Jessie," Edward said as he walked up behind Jessica and kissed her on the cheek. "Are you feeling any better?"

"I wasn't feeling bad to need to feel better," Jessica replied as she walked away and wiped the kitchen table.

Edward looked a little taken aback but continued. "I thought we might spend the day together doing something, what do you reckon?" he said.

"I've got plans today, I'm off out with Marie," Jessica said without looking at him.

"Oh," he said, he looked hurt.

"Jessica," Ellie said, "Edward's come all this way to see you, you can change your plans."

"But I haven't seen my sister in ages," Jessica protested.

"You've seen her all week. In any case I need Marie's help so you are free to go out," Ellie said.

"I thought I'd done my stint," Marie said.

"In this place there's a stint every day," Ellie said, "and if you're both here tomorrow could you cover lunchtime as I'm going out."

"I'm not heading back until Monday," Edward said. "I've booked a day off work. If you like I can help out too." He sounded quite enthusiastic.

"That would be great Edward, thank you," said Ellie.

Ellie made a cup of coffee and carried it back downstairs. She glanced around and realised she'd have to have a bit of a tidy up as the potential buyers were coming back for a second viewing next weekend. At least she'd have some extra staff next week.

As predicted the tea room was busy for most of the day. Marie proved a real asset and was soon taking orders, seating customers and even using the coffee machine.

"Thanks Marie," Ellie said as they closed up.

"I've actually really enjoyed it," Marie said. "I'm even looking forward to working here tomorrow."

"I'll miss you both when you're gone," Ellie said. "We must have a day out before you go back."

"How about tonight?" Marie said.

"I'd love to but I really need to get some sleep," Ellie said yawning. "I know it's early but I think I'll go straight to bed."

"You go on up and I'll clean up," said Marie. "You deserve a rest."

Ellie hugged her daughter. "Thanks again," she said.

14

Ellie opened the tea room door, looked up at the blue sky, closed her eyes and felt the warmth of the sun on her face. This was the first Sunday of the Easter holidays. Families had arrived in town yesterday and today they would be making the most of this glorious weather. She set up the tables outside, even here she liked to put out small vases of fresh flowers.

Pat had arrived early and Edward was already helping her in the kitchen. The girls were nowhere to be seen; another late night last night, at least they'd taken Edward with them.

Ellie walked back into the kitchen and turned on the urn.

"Thanks for helping out," Ellie said to Edward. "It's going to get a bit hectic later on."

"I've always fancied being a chef," he said, "well maybe not a chef but at least doing something like this."

"Have you had much experience?" Pat asked.

"Well I have cooked the occasional Sunday roast and I do a mean boeuf bourguignon," he said laughing.

"Maybe we should start with a few sandwich fillings and move onto the French cuisine this afternoon," Pat said.

"Hopefully the girls will be down before the customers arrive," Ellie said. "I would like to get away early enough to get changed. I'll probably get asked for drinks if I go into the pub like this," she continued indicating her black clothes and white apron.

As if on cue Jessica and Marie walked into the kitchen.

"Dressed and ready for action," Marie said saluting Ellie.

15

At eleven o'clock Ellie went upstairs to get changed, the tea room was busy but everyone seemed to be coping well. She'd already spent some time earlier deciding what to wear, she didn't want to give the impression she'd tried too hard and yet she wanted to make sure she looked smart. She had decided on a pair of smart jeans, a fitted t-shirt and a lightweight tweed jacket, although she probably wouldn't need the jacket. She looked at herself in the mirror. It had been a while since she'd been out with a man, this wasn't exactly a date but she still felt nervous.

"Mum, Michael's here," Marie called up the stairs.

"On my way," she said smoothing down a stray strand of hair before heading downstairs.

"Hi," Ellie said to Michael as she went into the tea room.

"Hi," Michael replied. "Ready?"

"Ready," Ellie said.

Ellie looked at Pat. "You've got my number if you need me, I'll only be up the road," she said.

"Go and enjoy yourself," Pat said. "We'll be fine."

Marie leaned towards Ellie and whispered in her ear. "And you've got my number if you need me," she said.

"Very funny," Ellie said as she walked out of the door.

"Bye," said Jessica, popping her head out of the kitchen.

Ellie and Michael walked towards the pub.

"It's such a lovely day," said Ellie. "Why don't we grab a coffee from across the road and have a walk in the Abbey Grounds instead?"

"Sounds good to me," said Michael.

Michael ordered two lattes and selected two slices of cake. "I guess this is a bit of a busman's holiday for you," he said.

"Not at all, good cake is good cake," Ellie said smiling.

They took their coffee, walked around the side of the church and followed the path towards the Roman wall.

"How did the party go?" Ellie asked.

"Great. Grace was blown away by the cake, I think I've become her favourite uncle," Michael said laughing. "Of course, that's not difficult as I'm her only uncle. The party was a real surprise. Grace knew we were taking her out so she got dressed up. We drove her to the village hall, it's still a bit far for her to walk, and when she walked in everyone let off party poppers and started singing Happy Birthday."

"She must mean a lot to you," Ellie said.

"I don't have any children myself, never been married, so yes Grace means a lot to me as does her mum. We're twins you see and to see her struggling so much after the accident was really hard," Michael said looking at Ellie.

"I have twin daughters and I often see how connected they are so I get what you mean. You said they had an accident," Ellie said.

"Yes, quite a few months back. A car slid on some mud, back in the autumn, and ploughed right into them. Grace was on the passenger side and took the full brunt. There were a few days when we were told she might not make it. Laura, my sister, just sat by her side hour after hour even though she was told to rest because of her own injuries. She had Grace quite late in life, she'd struggled to conceive and eventually had IVF so, whilst I'm sure all children are special, to Laura Grace was a real gift," Michael said. He pulled a cotton handkerchief from his pocket and wiped his eyes.

"What about Grace's father?" Ellie asked.

"He's in the army, he was serving away at the time, he was able to get back but it took a few days," Michael said. "As you know she pulled through. But that was just the start. Her leg had been shattered, there was talk of removing it, but after several operations and a long stint in hospital she's on the mend. She'll have to have check-ups and x-rays to make sure everything's okay as she grows but things are looking good."

Ellie put a hand on his arm. "Well I think she's really lucky to have you as an uncle," she said.

"Well that's me, what about you? You say you have

twins," Michael said.

"Yes, twin daughters, their father died when they were two so I moved here and opened the tea room. They're grown up now, both moved out even though they've both come back to visit this week. And now I've decided to sell up and do something different," Ellie said.

"I've only just met you and you're leaving," Michael said laughing.

"I'm not going far, just outside Cirencester." Ellie said.

"Can we do this again, soon?" Michael said.

"I'd like that," Ellie said. "Give me a ring."

Ellie finished her coffee and continued to walk around the grounds with Michael. When they reached the pond she threw a few crumbs to the ducks and thought briefly about her future. She was enjoying Michael's company but she wasn't sure if this was the right time to start a relationship, not that Michael had asked for one. Once the tea room was sold she wanted to spend more time with the girls and help Jessica with the baby, and then she wanted to travel. Although she was sure the occasional coffee wouldn't hurt.

"Penny for them," Michael said.

"Sorry, I was just thinking I need to get back to the tea room," Ellie said. "The girls seem to know what they're doing but I can't leave them for too long especially as this is a sort of holiday for them."

"Come on then," Michael said. "I won't persuade you to stay but only because I intend to repeat this in the very near future."

"I'm already looking forward to it," said Ellie.

****

Ellie said goodbye to Michael and walked back towards the tea room. She could see it was busy, all of the outside tables were taken. It would only take her ten minutes to dash upstairs, get changed and be ready to help out. Ellie decided to go in through the tea room door, at least she could assess the damage and work out where she was most needed.

The door was open, as she approached Marie came out carrying a tray of tea and cakes.

"Hi Mum," Marie said. "Did you have a good time? You haven't been gone that long."

"Hi," said Ellie surprised at how well organised everything seemed. "Yes, and no, I think. I decided to get back and give you a hand, I know how busy it gets."

"No need," said Marie as she put the tray on one of the tables. "All under control. Why don't you take the rest of the afternoon off."

"Thanks," Ellie said as she looked through the door and saw Jessica clearing a table ready for a waiting family. "But I'll still pop back down if that's alright."

16

Ellie liked to spend Sunday evenings making cakes and scones for the week ahead. Even though they baked every day she liked to start the week with plenty of stock. She'd left everyone upstairs watching TV, clearly exhausted from working in the tea room.

She sat on a stool with pencil in hand ready to write a list of the cakes she needed.

"Sorry Mum," said Jessica as she walked into the kitchen.

"For what, I thought we'd got over the moving thing," Ellie said.

"For just turning up and thinking you should always be there when I have a crisis," said Jessica.

"I will always be here," Ellie said smiling. "Are you having a crisis?"

"Maybe, I don't know," said Jessica sitting next to Ellie.

"What's really up, is it Edward?" said Ellie.

"Not really, he's just trying to make everything go well, take the pressure off me. The thing is I don't think I can cope. I really don't think I'm ready to have a baby," said Jessica.

Ellie looked at the tiny bump. "Whatever your doubts I don't think you have much choice," she said.

"Don't get me wrong I do want the baby but… what if I'm a terrible mother? What if I don't do as good a job as you? I'm not sure I have the faintest idea about what to do and, if I'm honest, I feel absolutely terrified," Jessica said twisting the edge of her shirt. "I don't know how you did it, two young children and a business, you seemed to manage with ease. Me, I can't even manage a day at work and summon up any energy to paint the nursery. I don't think I'm going to manage, especially when Edward has to go back to work. Can't I just come and live with you, you could help me, you know what to do."

"Oh Jessie, stop comparing yourself to others, least of all me," Ellie said. "You do realise it was all an illusion don't you? I didn't actually manage it that well at all, I just tried to get to the end of each day without any major disasters."

Jessica laughed, though she continued to twist the edge of her shirt. "But what if I'm a rubbish mum?" she said.

"You are going to be a great mum, trust me," Ellie said, putting her arm around her daughter. "Do you know when you were first born I looked at you both and worried how on earth I was going to look after the two of you. Life before you were born was so simple. I had a job but, as long as I did that, I could get up when I wanted, eat when I wanted and go to bed when I wanted. Then all of a sudden I had responsibilities. I couldn't lie in just because I felt like it, and I had to get to bed early just to make sure I had enough sleep to be able to get up at midnight, and four o'clock and six o'clock. But do you know what, I wouldn't have changed it for the world. Every time I looked at the two of you I felt like the luckiest person alive. Watching you both grow up just could not compare to what I thought I was giving up – the parties, late nights out with friends, Sunday mornings in bed - it was all fun but not a patch on the love I felt for you."

"But you seemed able to do everything," said Jessica.

"Seemed, maybe, but the reality was very different," Ellie said smiling at her daughter. "There were many days when I thought I was letting you both down and I often wondered why customers came back to the tea room considering how rough I felt. I certainly didn't look capable of making a cup of tea let alone run a tea room or bring up two children."

"I think you're exaggerating a bit Mum," said Jessica laughing. "All I can remember is you doing a great job. Lots of games, the occasional telling off for not doing our homework, and always being there when we needed you."

"And you'll do a great job," said Ellie. "If you have an off day, I'm not too far away. And you have Edward, don't cut him out, let him enjoy being a father. Your father, even if it was only for a brief period, took every opportunity to be with you. Allow Edward to share in the joys as well as the challenges."

Tears started to roll down Jessica's face.

Ellie held her tighter. "Look if it would help I could put off selling the tea room for a while," Ellie said.

"Maybe, no, I don't know, that wouldn't be fair," said Jessica wiping her eyes with a tissue. "It just seems that everything is changing so fast."

"I used to think that when you were growing up," Ellie said. "Remember, I'll only be a phone call away."

"Not if you go travelling," said Jessica, still sounding tearful even though she was smiling.

"I promise I won't go away, well not more than a few hours anyway, until you are settled with the baby, okay," said Ellie trying to reassure her daughter.

"Okay," said Jessica.

"Right, come on, help me get these scones made," said Ellie getting up.

"If it's alright with you I think I'll go and have that chat with Edward, maybe suggest we go and choose some paint for the nursery tomorrow," said Jessica.

Ellie smiled at her daughter. "I think that's a great idea," she said.

17

Ellie woke feeling refreshed; this weather showed no sign of breaking and the seasonal staff started today. Adam and Jo had worked for her before so they both knew what they were doing. Adam was at university and only worked during the holidays but Jo went to the local college and was happy to work weekends and the occasional weekday if it didn't clash with her lectures.

As she sat up she could hear voices downstairs, a bit early for Pat and she wasn't expecting the staff for another two hours. She threw some clothes on and went down to the tea room. Edward and Jessica were getting the place ready, they'd already changed the cloths and were filling the salt and pepper pots.

"Morning Mum," said Jessica

"I thought we had uninvited guests," said Ellie laughing.

"No, just thought we'd help out," said Jessica. "Well actually it was Edward who said we should help, he pointed out how busy you'd been."

Edward looked at Ellie. "Sorry if we worried you," he said.

"No, I could tell it was friendly voices," said Ellie.

"We're heading back in a couple of hours, so I thought I'd cook everyone breakfast before we go," Edward said. "We've already packed and we've left the room tidy ready for any viewings."

"Wow," said Ellie looking at Jessica. "Are you sure my daughter hasn't been abducted by aliens and replaced by an imposter?"

"Very funny Mum, I haven't been that bad, well maybe just a little, but…," Jessica said her words trailing off.

"I was only joking, you know it's always great to see you, in fact I'm hoping to see a lot more of you both now," Ellie said. "Maybe I can come and stay with you for a few days and then I can leave towels on the floor."

They all laughed.

"I'll just pop up to the butchers," said Edward, "and pick up some bacon and sausages. Then I'll do that breakfast."

Edward cooked up a fantastic full English. Not only had he bought bacon and sausages he'd picked up some mushrooms, tomatoes and black pudding. The kitchen looked remarkably tidy considering he'd had every hot plate in use and several pans on the go.

Ellie looked at Jessica. "It's been wonderful seeing you even if we haven't had much chance to spend time together. But that is going to change," she said.

She then turned and looked at Marie. "If you're staying for a couple more days perhaps we could go out one evening," she said smiling.

"That would be great Mum," said Marie "I'm here until Wednesday then I have to get back, I've got some prep to do for next week."

Edward collected the suitcases and brought them into the tea room. "Ready?" he said looking at Jessica.

"Yes," said Jessica. "See you soon Mum, very soon."

"Don't worry," Ellie said putting her hand on Jessica's arm. "Even if it takes a few months to sell the tea room I'll make time to come to Bristol, if need be I'll get some extra help."

"What you, let someone else take control," said Jessica.

"I think that over this last week I've said goodbye and moved on just a little," Ellie said looking around the tea room. She stared at the photos, paintings and prints on the wall, all were of the local area and most were by local artists. In the early days she used to wander down to the market and buy the occasional picture, it had helped her build a connection with the area. Nowadays artists tended to come to her and ask if they could display their work, this worked well as it gave her a constant supply of new paintings. She'd probably select one or two paintings to take with her but most she'd leave behind.

Jessica gave Ellie a hug. "Thanks Mum, for everything," she said. "We'd better get going if we're going to do some shopping." She turned to Marie, "Thanks for a great week, we must get together more often, I've really enjoyed myself."

Edward picked up the cases. "Bye," he said following Jessica out of the door, "and I have to say I've had a good weekend too."

Ellie watched as they walked up the road and rounded the corner towards their car. Later today she'd definitely sort out staffing so she could spend more time with both of her daughters.

Ellie turned to Marie. "Would you like to see the cottage I'm buying? We could go after lunch," she said.

"I'd like that a lot," said Marie.

18

After lunch Ellie hung up her apron and went into the kitchen. "I'll be back before closing," Ellie said to Pat, "any major problems ring me and I'll come straight back."

"What exactly do you think could go wrong?" Pat said smiling. "We'll be fine,"

"I know but with this weather you might get a late rush," Ellie said.

"If we do we'll manage," said Pat.

Ellie drove the car off the driveway and made her way out of Cirencester.

Marie pointed out some daffodils that were in full bloom. "This area is beautiful in the spring," she said.

"It's beautiful any time of year," Ellie said. "I love this weather, but I think I like winter best, especially when it snows."

"Yes, and of course Christmas is wonderful - snow on the trees, clear nights with lots of stars, lights everywhere, the little Christmas market in Cirencester and the big one in Bath," said Marie.

"And don't forget the magical lights at the Arboretum," said Ellie.

"How could I?" said Marie. "The annual walk around the trees, hot chocolate and Christmas carols."

"We should go again this year, all of us," said Ellie. Ellie paused briefly. "Is something up Marie? It's unlike you to take time off work."

"I don't know," Marie said. "I love my job, but sometimes I feel a little isolated."

"What, in London?" Ellie said. London was the place Marie had longed to be even before she'd finished university. She'd said it was where it was all happening. Maybe it was just in her blood, her father had been born in London and saw no reason to live anywhere else.

"Yes, I've got friends," said Marie. "But when Jessica

announced she was having a baby I felt a little detached from it all. I couldn't get to see her for three weeks. I think I felt a little homesick and perhaps more than a little envious that you and Jessica have your lives under control and... you seem close to each other."

"Oh Marie," said Ellie reaching out to her. "I'm close to both of you. And as for things being under control, well maybe we are just better at being swans, you know, serene on top but absolute chaos going on underneath."

Marie laughed.

"So what are you going to do?" Ellie said.

"Go back," Marie said. "I'm actually starting to miss my job, I was even working on my new project last night. I'm not sure about living in London though, maybe I need to move a bit further this way and commute. We'll see."

"When I'm glad you love your job, you've worked hard for it." Ellie said. "There was a time when I worried how you'd cope if you didn't get the job you wanted. Of course there was no need to worry, you were always going to be just fine."

"I am going to make time to come back a little more often though, if that's okay with you," Marie said.

"Of course it is, I'd be over the moon," Ellie said. "And I can come and see you more often once I've moved, there's some great deals on the trains and I can go direct from Kemble."

Ellie pulled into a carpark next to a village hall. "This is it," she said, "well the village anyway. Let's have a wander then I'll show you the house."

They walked past a small cluster of houses, a village shop with a Post Office, a pub and a church. They turned up a lane and Ellie stopped.

"This is it," Ellie said, pointing to a honey coloured stone cottage with a sold sign outside.

"Wow," said Marie. "I can see why you fell in love with it. The garden is beautiful, you can see it'll be a riot of colour in the summer."

"And that's just the front, the back garden has a

vegetable plot and a small orchard. Perhaps we can fix up a swing in one of the trees," Ellie said. "There's only two bedrooms so I'll have to sell some of the furniture but the kitchen is huge so I should be able to do some serious baking."

"Well I for one can't wait to visit," Marie said.

Ellie hugged her daughter. "I'm glad you like it," Ellie said smiling. "We ought to get back though, I want to see Adam and Jo before they leave today."

19

"Hi Pat," said Ellie as she walked back into the tea room. "How is everything?"

"Absolutely fine, the staff have been fantastic, really looking after our customers," Pat said smiling at Adam and Jo.

"Great, I'll help finish up," said Ellie.

"Before you do you've got visitors, they're in the back room," said Pat.

Ellie was puzzled, she wasn't expecting anyone and the estate agent hadn't booked in any more viewings. Marie followed her through the hallway.

"Jessica, Edward what are you doing back, is everything okay?" said Ellie.

"Yes, Mum, well sort of," said Jessica looking a little nervous. "We got back and we were going to go to the DIY store but, well, my heart just wasn't in it. I couldn't get enthusiastic about paint colours or furniture or anything."

"Oh, Jessica," said Ellie.

"No, it's alright, we went out to lunch instead and we talked, a lot," said Jessica twisting the strap of her handbag. "You know I've been feeling, well, quite nervous about having the baby and, when I actually stopped to listen, turns out Edward is quite jealous of me getting to look after him or her so we had a long talk and made some decisions."

"Let me guess," said Ellie smiling and feeling a little relieved. "You're going to go back to work and Edward's going to stay at home."

"Not exactly," said Jessica twisting the strap even tighter.

Ellie looked from Jessica to Edward, they both looked quite nervous.

After what seemed like an age but was more like a minute Edward spoke up. "We'd like to buy the tea room. Obviously we've got to sell our house in Bristol and of course we'd need to secure the loan but if we can get it sorted we'd like to put in an offer," Edward said without pausing.

Marie clapped her hands. "That's a fantastic idea," she said, "it's not too far for me to drive and I'd get to see my nephew or niece as often as I like."

Ellie looked from Jessica to Edward. "Are you sure you know what you're letting yourself in for?" she asked.

"Probably not," said Jessica. "But what better place to bring up a baby," she looked at Edward, "or two. We'd get to share looking after our little one and you'd be close by, that's when you're not swanning off all over the world."

"Oh Jessica, Marie, you know I'll always be here for you, whatever happens," Ellie said laughing. "Even if I do have to Skype from some remote island."

Pat walked in with a tray of teacups and a pot of English Breakfast tea. Edward stood up and poured tea into each of the cups. As he handed them around Ellie noticed her mobile light up. The text message read Are you free Thursday night? Michael. Ellie smiled. She had said it was time for some changes. She looked down at her phone and replied - Yes.

Marie picked up her cup. "A toast," she said, "to the end of an era."

Ellie raised her cup. "And to new beginnings," she said.

"To new beginnings," they all replied.

The End

Book Two

The Vintage Tea Room 2
room for a small one

Lily Wells

1

Jessica smiled as she felt the warming rays of the morning sun across her face. Monday morning, their first day in their new home. She rolled onto her side and pulled the duvet over her shoulders. If she kept her eyes closed she could hang on to the last threads of her dream, she couldn't actually remember much but she knew that Edward had been part of it and that made her feel good. She felt she'd come home. Returning to Cirencester had been the best decision they'd made, it felt good to be back in her old bed and even better to be sharing it with Edward. She placed one hand on her now large bump, when baby finally arrived their life here would be perfect. "Not long now," she whispered as she moved her hand to where she could feel a kick.

It was a few minutes before she opened her eyes and caught sight of the clock. The red numbers almost screamed at her – 8:41. Their first day as new owners of the tea room and she was late. Jessica maneuvered herself, and her bump, into a sitting position, she slowly swung her legs over the side of the bed, pushed herself up onto her feet and pulled on her dressing gown. She caught a glimpse of herself in the mirror, she definitely wasn't one of those elegantly pregnant women, more of a mother duck, she sighed as she waddled down the stairs. The sun was already streaming through the window forming little pools of brightness on the wooden floor.

"Edward, we're late, we can't open late on our first day," Jessica shouted as she went into the tea room.

Edward walked out of the kitchen and smiled. "Thinking of introducing a new uniform or just having a pyjama day?" he said.

Jessica tried to pull her gown together, it didn't quite meet in the middle, and tied the belt. "I'm being serious," she said. "Why did you let me oversleep?"

"Because you needed it, we've had a busy few days moving in and you have to rest," he said.

"I know, but not today," she replied and started walking towards the kitchen.

Edward gently grabbed her by the shoulders and turned her around, "No you don't," he said. "I'm guessing you haven't eaten yet."

"Not yet," she said.

"Then sit down and I'll bring you something," he said making his way back to the kitchen.

"We haven't got time," she said.

"Then we'll make time, sit," he shouted from the kitchen as he filled a pan with hot water from the urn.

Jessica sat at the nearest table and looked around, none of the tables were ready for opening. The tablecloths hadn't been changed, there were no fresh flowers, and the salt and pepper pots didn't look like they'd been filled.

"Edward, what would Mum think, I can't even manage to get things right on our first day. She'll think I'm a failure and she'd be right," she said frowning.

"She'd be very proud of you and tell you to stop worrying. I'll prepare a couple of tables then do the others after we open," Edward replied as he carried a plate towards Jessica.

"Stop sounding so in control," she said trying to look annoyed but failing to control her smile.

"Eat your breakfast," he said putting poached eggs on toast in front of her. "Then get dressed, and no rushing."

Jessica cut into one of her eggs, the yellow yolk ran out across her toast just the way she liked it. As she took her first bite the doorbell jangled, she looked up to see Pat walk in dressed in her usual black uniform.

"Morning," said Pat. "All ready to go?" she asked.

"Not quite," said Jessica blushing. "But we're on the case." She stood up.

"You sit back down," said Edward firmly. "I've turned on the coffee machine, the urn is ready, and I am just about the check the tablecloths. The flowers can wait until after Jessica has had breakfast," continued Edward as he turned towards Pat.

Pat looked at Jessica. "Been running around all morning and forgotten to eat?" asked Pat smiling.

"Something like that," said Jessica. "Actually it was more like I overslept and Edward made me eat first."

"I've told her no work until after breakfast. If we get any early customers I'm sure we can cope," said Edward sternly.

"Of course we can, this time of year it eases off a little, kids are back at school and the summer rush is over. I really enjoy autumn," said Pat as she grabbed an apron.

Jessica stood up again and picked up her plate, "I'll eat upstairs, I'm feeling a bit in the way," she said.

"Don't be daft, this is your place now, you sit down, we've got a while before opening," said Pat as she headed towards the kitchen.

The bell on the door jangled again.

"Morning Margaret," said Edward smiling at their first customer.

"Morning, I wasn't sure if you'd remember me. I know I'm early and you're not open yet but I thought I'd catch the early bus in and have a quick look before the grand opening to see if you'd made any changes," said Margaret looking around the tea room. As usual Margaret looked smart with perfectly applied make-up. If it wasn't for the time of day Jessica would have thought she'd come straight from the hair salon.

"No, it's exactly as you last saw it," said Edward.

"I'm glad, this is such a lovely place it would be a shame to see it all modern," said Margaret as she smiled at Jessica.

Jessica blushed as she finished her eggs, she guessed she must look quite a sight, over eight months pregnant, no make-up and in her PJs. She was sure her mum never got caught out like this.

"Would you like a tea, Margaret," Edward asked guiding her towards a window seat.

"That would be lovely, if it's not too early," said Margaret.

"We're not quite ready but if you don't mind us tidying around you then no problem. Your usual, Earl Grey and a cake?" he asked.

"That would be good. It's nice to see some things don't change, you're going to do just fine here," she said as she sat at the table.

Jessica watched Edward easily and naturally take over, he made the tea and laid a tray for Margaret whilst Pat went into the kitchen and started to prepare some sandwich fillings. She frowned as she stood up. This hadn't been the start she'd imagined, although it had all gone smoothly even though she'd overslept. And yet something bothered her - everything seemed to be on autopilot and it didn't need her input. She didn't exactly feel in the way but she didn't feel part of things either. This might be a successful business and a great place for them to bring up their baby but it was still her mum's place; she wanted to make it her place. Perhaps they could change the name - Jess and Ed - that sounded like a happening place. Well maybe not but she needed to do something different and soon.

Jessica finished her breakfast and carried her plate into the kitchen.

"I'll see you in a few minutes," she said to Edward.

Edward handed her a cup of coffee. "Take this with you," he said, "and don't rush."

Jessica brought the cup close to her nose and breathed deeply, if there was one thing she loved it was the aroma of freshly brewed coffee, especially the first cup of the day. This might be a tea room, and she usually drank tea with her mum, but this was one pleasure she was not giving up.

"Thank-you," she said leaning forward and kissing his cheek.

The rest of the day went smoothly. Not that Jessica expected anything else. Lunchtime was busy but manageable, Pat restocked the kitchen with sandwich fillings, Edward managed the customers with ease, he was a natural both in the tea room and in the kitchen. As for herself, she made coffee, prepared the bills and generally busied herself. Shortly after lunch Jessica decided to take a short rest.

"Take your time," Edward said as he cleared a table, "we can manage."

"I know," she said. And that was what was bothering her, she wasn't needed.

2

Jessica woke early on Tuesday morning; she wasn't going to have a repeat of yesterday. She lay in bed for a while listening to the dawn chorus, this was one of the reasons she had wanted to move back, those few moments when she felt peaceful. She'd enjoyed the buzz of Bristol but there never seemed to be a break from the noise, there was always someone doing something. She opened her eyes as Edward stirred beside her.

"Happy?" he said turning to face her.

"Very," she replied, smiling.

"Ready for the second day of the rest of our lives?" he said.

"You bet," she replied as she sat up.

Edward plumped up the pillows behind her.

"You spoil me," she said.

"Gotta keep you fit and healthy," he said laughing and gently patting her stomach.

"Too right," she said giving him a friendly punch on the arm. "Else you'll be doing all the work on your own."

After breakfast she wandered downstairs. The baby seemed to have shifted a little and she wasn't feeling so uncomfortable. Edward was showering so she decided to make a start getting the tea room ready. She might not be able to move very fast but she could change the cloths and arrange the flowers. This place held a lot of memories for Jessica. Although, despite everything being familiar, she hadn't really looked that closely before. When they bought the place they'd bought it lock, stock and barrel so everything was as it had always been, yet, if asked, she couldn't have told anyone that the tablecloths were covered in flowers, now she looked she noted there was quite a few different patterns such as roses, lavender and marigolds. She looked at the photos and painting on the walls, she could see why her mum had loved them, mostly scenes of local places she knew well, places they had visited together as a family. She stared at one for a while, the arboretum, the reds, umbers and golds portrayed an autumn scene. She took a little time to notice the detail, the different colours of the branches, the light and shadows, and the way the artist drew the eye through the trees to something promised, but not quite seen. Jessica preferred paintings to photographs as, for her, they captured a feeling rather than a moment. This painting stirred the feeling she had when kicking fallen leaves and jumping in muddy puddles - a childish pleasure - she felt a smile grow across her face. They had spent many a late afternoon just running through the trees, playing hide and seek and enjoying the freedom. She looked down at her bump. "I think we'll spend many an afternoon there too," she said.

By the time Edward joined her she had finished preparing the tables and had started polishing the cutlery. He seemed to enjoy working in the kitchen so she'd left that for him.

"And what time do you call this," Jessica said putting her hands on her hips.

"Very funny," Edward said coming over and placing his hand on her stomach, "and good morning to both of you, too."

"Now I'm feeling a bit jealous, I want your attention all to myself," she said kissing him on the cheek.

The bell jangled and Pat walked in.

"I think it might take me a while to get used to working with a couple of lovebirds," she said. "I'll start making some more cakes this morning. Is it the same as usual?"

"Yes," said Edward, "we must keep the customers happy."

Jessica frowned." Edward, have you got a minute," she said.

"Of course, what is it, is the baby okay?" he asked looking concerned.

"Yes, the baby's fine. Look I know we've only just moved in but I really want us to put our own stamp on the tea room, make it our own," she said.

"It will be, I've no doubt you'll do just as good a job as your mum especially as we've got Pat to show us the ropes," he said. He placed a hand on Jessica's arm.

"That's just it," she said sitting down at one of the tables, "I don't want to do 'as good a job' as mum, I want to do it our way."

"I get it, you want to come up with some of your own cakes," he said.

The doorbell jangled again. Margaret had arrived.

"Morning, Margaret," said Edward turning towards the door.

"You seem to have settled in perfectly," Margaret said.

Edward took her coat and led her to her usual window seat. "Jessica's thinking of introducing some new cakes," he said.

"Nothing too fancy I hope," Margaret said, "and don't get rid of the lemon sponge, that's my favourite."

Edward smiled. "Don't worry, I'm sure it won't be anything too radical," he said as he went to make the tea.

Jessica caught his arm as he walked by. "We'll talk later," she said, frowning, "and stop making fun of me."

"I wasn't aware I was, I think your idea is great," he said.

"But that wasn't my idea, it was yours," she said.

****

By lunchtime most of the tables were taken. Jessica took orders and delivered the teas and lunches. As she squeezed between a couple of chairs she thought she'd soon be too big to do this job, or perhaps she'd have to take some of the tables out.

"Afternoon," said Jessica as a young couple walked in. "Table for two?"

"Yes please," the young girl said, "what do you have for lunch?"

"We can do an afternoon tea with a range of sandwiches

and cakes or you can have just the sandwiches. We have all the fillings on the menu as well as our special - smoked salmon with cream cheese and chives," Jessica replied.

"What type of bread do you have?" the girl asked.

Jessica looked a little puzzled. "Brown and white," she said.

The girl smiled. "The afternoon tea sounds wonderful, we'll have that," she said.

"Good choice," said Jessica, "and thank-you."

"What for," asked the girl.

"For giving me a great idea," said Jessica as she headed back towards the kitchen. She had to talk to Edward soon.

****

The end of the day couldn't come soon enough for Jessica, the steady stream of customers meant that she had no time to speak to Edward during the afternoon. As closing time came and the last of the customers finished their late afternoon tea Jessica couldn't hold off any longer. She made two cups of coffee and put them on a table near the kitchen.

"Edward, can we talk, I have an idea," she said.

"Of course, when we've finished up we can chat over supper," he said.

"I can't wait until then, I need to talk to you now," she said. She noticed Edward's look of concern. "And it's not the baby so stop worrying."

"Are you sure this can't wait," he said as he handed a coat to the last customer.

Jessica followed the customers and bolted the door behind them. "I'm sure," she said. "Sit down."

"Sounds ominous," said Edward sitting at the table and taking a sip of his coffee.

"Earlier, I said I wanted us to make our mark," Jessica said joining him at the table.

"Yes, and I agreed," said Edward.

"But you didn't even hear my idea," Jessica said.

"New cakes, maybe even different tea blends, and perhaps coffees," Edward said.

Jessica picked up the corner of the tablecloth and started to twist it in her hands. "No," she said, a few tears were forming in the corner of her eyes, "you suggested that."

"Then what were you going to say?" Edward asked.

"Well, to be honest I didn't have an idea. I was hoping we could come up with one," she said.

"Over coffee?" Edward asked.

"You're making fun of me again," she said.

"I'm sorry, I don't mean to. It's just I think we should settle in first, get to know the ropes, especially with the baby due so soon, before we do anything major," he said.

"I don't want to settle in, if we settle in this will always be mum's tea room and I want it to be ours. And the baby's not due for ages," she replied the tears starting to fall down her cheeks.

"But we can't just abandon everything here, we'd lose all our customers," he said.

"I don't want to abandon anything, I want to add something, don't you get it. A bit like adding a modern extension to an old castle," she said.

"I get it now," Edward said smiling, "we need to talk to planning."

"What?" she said.

"About this extension," Edward said.

Jessica picked up a napkin and threw it at him

"You think you're so funny, but I'm being serious," she said sounding calmer.

"I know you are, that's what scares me. What do you have in mind?" Edward asked.

"Like I said, this morning I didn't have an idea but it came to me when I was talking to a customer at lunchtime," she said sounding excited. "We could make bread, proper Artisan bread."

Edward put his coffee cup on the table. "Do you know how?" he asked.

"No, but we could learn, it can't be that hard," she said losing none of her enthusiasm. "We could offer lots of different types - olive bread, cranberry at Christmas, and oils for dipping."

"Whoa," said Edward holding up his hand.

"I'm going to make this happen," she said.

"You will, but I don't want you to be disappointed if it doesn't happen overnight," he said taking her hand in his. "Let's start with the basics and see if we can make a plain white loaf first. What do you need?"

"I'm not sure," said Jessica getting her phone out of her pocket. "I'll look it up." She looked at Edward. "The internet is as good a place as any."

"I know," he said, "make a list and I'll go shopping tomorrow."

Jessica took a sip of her coffee, it had started to cool, "I think we have a plan," she said.

"We have an idea, we still need a plan," said Edward smiling at her.

3

Wednesday had been another busy day. Once all the customers had left Jessica began to clear the kitchen, she started to appreciate how hard her mum had worked all these years. As she finished wiping down the worktops Edward walked in and placed a bag of flour and yeast on the table. "All local produce, and the yeast came from the local bakery, they were happy to donate some," he said. "What would you like me to do?"

"Cook tea," Jessica said. "As far as I can make out this first stage should take about an hour then I have to leave it to rise." She kissed Edward on the cheek. "Thank-you. I'll be up soon."

Jessica checked the recipe and then carefully weighed the flour and tipped it into the mixing bowl. She opened the yeast, the smell hit her and made her heave, the morning sickness had never entirely left her and it didn't confine itself to mornings. She crumbled it into the flour. Finally, she added softened butter, salt and a little sugar. Jessica put the bowl onto the mixer with the dough hooks and turned it on. Once done she covered the bowl with a tea towel. The instructions had just said to leave the dough in a warm place to rise, she hoped the kitchen wasn't too hot.

Jessica set the timer on her phone for forty-five minutes. She smiled as she imagined customers choosing their favourite bread and maybe even making requests for new recipes. She took one last look at her dough before going upstairs.

Edward had prepared a chicken salad. "I made the dressing myself," he said, grinning, "using a recipe from your mum."

Jessica looked at her plate of food, it looked really appealing with the spinach, tomatoes, carrots and cucumber layered on the plate and the lightly browned chicken pieces on top, there were even a few croutons.

She took a mouthful; it did taste good. "I think you

could add some salads to go with our bread," she said. "This could be the start of a whole new direction for the tea room."

"Good idea," he said, "but I think I need to learn a bit more first, rustling up a meal for two is a bit different from feeding a tea room full of customers."

"You just need a bigger bowl," Jessica said laughing.

"At this rate I think I'll need a bigger kitchen," he said.

As she finished her meal Jessica's alarm went off.

"Time to go," she said, "stage two."

Jessica went back downstairs. She tipped the dough onto the floured worktop and started to gently knead it. The instructions had stated that she had to firmly knock the air out of it, she tried to apply a bit more pressure. She thought she'd really enjoy this part but it made her arms ache, probably because her bump meant she couldn't get close to the worktop and she had to lean awkwardly. As she worked she felt the baby give a kick, a real hard kick, she almost called out with surprise. This little bundle was definitely going to make sure he or she wasn't forgotten.

She shaped the dough into two loaf shaped mounds and placed them onto baking trays; she'd need to buy proper tins if she was going to do this properly. She covered the shaped dough and put it on one side to rise. After an hour, most of which she spent surfing the internet on her phone to find different bread recipes, she put the loaves into the oven and set the timer for thirty-five minutes.

The smell of freshly baking bread filled the room, what could be better. Yes, this was definitely going to be their thing – Mum had her tea and cakes, and she would have her bread. She looked around the kitchen, it was a decent size with two good sized ovens but they'd have to think carefully about how they managed the space when they baked, it wasn't big enough for them all to work in it once. Perhaps they could have a schedule, one day cakes, the next bread. But she did want her bread to be fresh every day. Maybe she could get up early and make the bread first thing, that way it would be really fresh.

The timer buzzed, Jessica turned off the oven, put on the

oven gloves, removed the tray and placed it on the worktop. The bread was a golden brown and smelt delicious, the crust was smoother and shinier than she'd expected but it still looked good. When she thought it had cooled enough she took the bread knife from the rack and tried to cut into the bread. The knife only dented the crust, she had to saw at it in order to break the surface. She picked up the loaf and pulled it apart, it was a heavy doughy mess. This was not how her bread should look, she had expected a light, fluffy texture with a crisp crust. Instead the bread looked chewy and, as for the crust, she didn't think she could even eat it.

Edward walked into the kitchen. "If smell is anything to go by this is going to taste amazing," he said.

"Go away," Jessica said sobbing, "it's awful, nothing like I expected it to be, I can't even bake a loaf of bread. How am I going to run this place and bring up a baby?"

Edward put his arm around her. "Remember you won't be doing it all by yourself, we're in this together," he said.

"I know, but it doesn't look like I'll be much help, I don't seem to be good at any of it," she said still sobbing.

"This is your first attempt, we just need more practice," Edward said putting his arm around her.

"I think this will take a lot more than practice," she said poking at the bread. "I followed the instructions exactly."

"Don't be so hard on yourself. I'm sure the next one will be much better," Edward said.

"That's easy for you to say," said Jessica.

"Most things are easy to say," Edward said pulling off a chunk of bread and popping it into his mouth. "It actually tastes okay you know. Try it."

Jessica tasted a small piece. "I don't think we could sell this. I bet you could do better. Perhaps you should make it next time," she said.

"Why don't we do it together?" he said. "It might be a bit quieter tomorrow."

"I really want to make this work," she said.

"And we will," said Edward kissing her on the cheek. "Just give it some time."

4

The late summer sun had brought plenty of visitors to the town and by lunchtime the tea room was full. Jessica was starting to feel tired and knew she'd have to take a break soon however she didn't want to leave Edward and Pat on their own. Perhaps they needed to get some additional help.

She sighed as the doorbell jangled again.

"I'm sorry," she said as she started to turn towards the door, "but there will be a little wait."

"Even for me," a familiar voice answered.

"Marie," cried Jessica attempting to rush towards her sister although it turned into more of a waddle. She flung her arms around Marie.

"Wow, you've certainly grown," Marie said smiling and stepping back to pat the bump.

"I know," said Jessica. "Less than a month to go, and that's if the little one arrives on time."

"I think you need to start counting in weeks, or even days. It's quite a bit less than a month," Marie said laughing.

Jessica spotted the suitcase near the door. "Are you staying?" asked Jessica. Her face lit up.

"If that's alright," said Marie. "I know you have just moved in but I thought I could give you a bit of a hand. I don't want to intrude though."

"Of course you can stay, you can have your old room. Mum left everything in it so it should feel just like home," she said.

"I thought maybe you'd have decorated ready for the new arrival," said Marie.

"Not yet, we've only been in a few days. I know Mum would have been happy for us to decorate over the summer but we seemed to be so busy, we haven't even bought a cot but we have a bit of time yet," said Jessica as she cleared some plates from an empty table.

"I think you'd better get a move on, you look ready to

drop right now," said Marie raising her eyebrows.

Jessica laughed. "And you mentioned lending a hand, could you start like," she paused, "now," she said.

"Of course, I'll pop my case in the hall," said Marie. "You might need to remind me what to do though."

"It'll be good to have a chat later," said Jessica. "Then I can tell you about my idea."

"Sounds intriguing," said Marie, as she grabbed an apron and started to clear a table.

Jessica and Marie spent the rest of lunchtime serving the customers. It was after three before it started to get a bit quieter.

Edward came out of the kitchen. "Take a break," he said to them both, "we can manage for a while."

"Quick," said Jessica grabbing Marie by the arm, "he's a hard taskmaster and might change his mind."

"You're right," said Edward as he followed them both up the stairs, "the only reason I'm carrying up your coffees is to make sure you're back within thirty minutes."

"I don't know how you put up with him," said Marie as she ran up the last few steps.

"Well come on then, what's the big idea?" asked Marie as they sat in the kitchen and sipped their coffee.

"I want to specialise in breads, you know lots of different types, olive bread, farmhouse, I've got loads of ideas," said Jessica sounding very excited.

"Very trendy. Do you think your customers will like it?" said Marie.

"I hope so, or rather I hope it will attract one or two new customers," said Jessica. "We'll still keep everything we have now with the bread as an addition, something new, something that will make it ours."

"You look a bit worried," said Marie.

"It's just that some of the customers keep saying they like things the way they are, and I'm not sure what Mum will think," said Jessica twisting a paper napkin in her hands.

"Mum will be fine, she'll love the idea, and the customers

will soon get used to it," said Marie. "When are you hoping to start - next spring?"

"Now. There's no point waiting. I was going to give it another go tonight, last night's effort didn't exactly turn out as planned," said Jessica.

"Or maybe we could go out instead, that's if you're up to it, not too tired," said Marie smiling at her sister. "If we go now we can have a late lunch or early dinner, I'm sure somewhere will be serving food."

"Well I am tired but not too tired. And I guess one more night before I try to bake bread again won't hurt. They've just done out the place in the courtyard. Perhaps we could eat there," said Jessica. "I'll just text Edward, it's a long walk back downstairs, and then I'll get ready." She took her phone out of her pocket.

"Will he want to come, with us?" asked Marie.

"Maybe, but I want to catch up with you, I haven't seen you all summer," Jessica said. "And it's quite early so he'll want to clear up and get ready for tomorrow. We must get better at meeting up, especially when you become an auntie."

"Don't worry, you won't be able to get rid of me once you've had the baby," Marie said.

5

Jessica and Marie wandered down the Market Place towards a little courtyard area. The Indian summer continued to provide bright sunshine and unseasonal warmth. Jessica had always loved this area, the different styles of buildings from the honey coloured stone to the timber frames and a few more modern additions which probably wouldn't get through planning now. She loved to while away an hour just browsing the shops, especially the small department store with its quirky layout and small rooms. She could feel herself flagging, as much as she loved this weather she wished it would cool down just a little. As they passed the Corn Hall they noticed a sign for a craft market inside.

"Quick look," said Marie.

They walked through to the large room at the back, the building still had that feel of being an important trading place although it was now divided into smaller shops. Jessica absently picked up a hand carved wooden sheep and lamb.

"Over here," called Marie.

Jessica put down the wooden animals and went over to the stall where Marie waited. The table was laid out with baby clothes and teddy bears.

"Do you want to get a few things," asked Marie.

"Perhaps later, I'm quite hungry, and I want to hear about everything you've been doing this summer," said Jessica as she started to walk away.

"I'm beginning to think you're in denial," said Marie.

"About what?" answered Jessica looking puzzled.

"About having a baby," she said.

Jessica looked down at her bump. "You could be right," she said laughing. "If you hadn't pointed it out I wouldn't have noticed."

"You know what I mean," said Marie. "You have to get ready sometime."

"I know," said Jessica, "and I will. Just not right now.

Come on, it's just around the corner."

The little restaurant was painted white and had a flagstone floor. Despite being in the Cotswolds it had a continental feel. At the far end was a pizza oven, Jessica stood for a while watching as a freshly cooked pizza was taken out of the oven and cut into slices before being carried to a couple sat nearby. It smelt wonderful.

"Table for two," a voice cut into her thoughts.

"Yes please," replied Marie.

They were shown to a little table in an inglenook. The waiter handed them a menu and took their drinks order.

"They make and cook all the pizzas to order, you can even make your own if you like," said Jessica.

"Sounds fun, are you going to try one." said Marie.

"I have to say I go from ravenous to can't eat a thing in a matter of moments but I'm definitely going to order one, they'll box up any we leave," said Jessica.

"Well I fancy the ham and mushroom pizza with one of those beetroot salads," said Marie.

"I'll go for roasted veg," said Jessica, "my mouth is watering just looking at the pictures."

Jessica and Marie watched their pizzas being made up and placed in the oven, before long they were brought to the table. Jessica picked up a piece, strings of melted cheese hung down from the sides, she used her fingers to try and wrap it around the slice.

"Edward told me I'd find you here," said a woman approaching the table.

"Mum," said Jessica and Marie together.

"What are you doing here? I thought you were away for a few more days," said Jessica.

"I didn't want to miss the big event," said Ellie smiling.

"We opened Monday," said Jessica, "we just unlocked the door, no grand opening," said Jessica.

"No, I meant the baby," said Ellie.

"Don't worry there's ages yet," said Jessica.

Ellie pulled up a chair, scanned the menu and ordered a

blueberry smoothie.

"So, what are you two chatting about?" said Ellie.

"Just catching up," said Jessica.

"Jessica has been telling me about her idea for the tea room," said Marie winking at Jessica.

Jessica shook her head and look down at her food, she didn't want to share this idea with her mum just yet.

"Sounds interesting, fill me in," said Ellie.

"It's only an idea," said Jessica.

"It's a great idea and you're going to start soon I believe," said Marie.

Jessica looked at her mum, "I know you have built a really great business but I was hoping to add a little bit of me to it," she said twisting the crust off her pizza. "I was thinking of baking breads, that's if you don't mind."

"Why should I mind, it's yours, if you and Edward want to turn it into a nightclub then that's up to you," she said laughing.

"I wasn't thinking of going that far," Jessica said looking up, "I just don't want to let you down."

"You could never let me down," said Ellie reaching across and holding Jessica's hand, "I'll always be proud of you, both of you. It's your tea room now so make it yours."

Marie looked at Jessica. "Customers might say they don't like change but they also like to try new things," she said. "You and Edward complement each other perfectly, he keeps it all calm and settled whilst you add the zing. Everyone will be happy and the place will continue to thrive. And, it's important you enjoy it, so just go for it. And I for one can't wait to try your bread."

"Thanks, both of you, it means a lot," said Jessica.

"And whilst we're on the subject of making the place your own Edward tells me you are still in your old room and you don't have a nursery ready yet," said Ellie.

"The room is fine and all we need to do is buy a cot," said Jessica.

"And a pram. And bedding, and…," said Ellie counting

on her fingers.

"I know, I know, I'll get it done," said Jessica.

"Sorry, I didn't mean to fuss," said Ellie. "I think I'm just a bit excited, first grandchild and all that."

"I've got an idea." said Marie, "I'm down for a few days so why don't I help decorate Mum's room, I mean the main bedroom, for you and Edward - a house warming gift."

"That's a great idea," said Ellie. "I can help too. We'll go and get some wallpaper and wall paint, I freshened up all the paintwork earlier in the year so it shouldn't be too much work."

"What colours do you like," said Marie sounding all excited.

"It's a lovely idea but I'm not sure how I feel about moving into Mum's room," said Jessica.

"It's not my room, I have a new room, and anyway what are you going to do, lock it up and leave it empty?" said Ellie.

"I don't know, I haven't given it much thought," replied Jessica as she ate the last of her pizza.

"What was it you said earlier?" said Marie. "You want to put your stamp on the place, well start with the bedroom. You'll love it."

"Marie's right, it's your home," said Ellie, she paused, "and your business, so start treating it like yours."

Jessica smiled. "You're both right, of course. I can't wait to get started," she said.

"Come on," said Marie after she had paid the bill, "the homestore is still open so let's have some fun."

"I'm always amazed that for a small town Cirencester has some great shops," said Jessica. She stopped briefly to catch her breath.

"You okay?" asked Ellie.

"Yes, fine, just slowing down a bit," said Jessica.

They stopped and looked through the windows. From the outside the store had a traditional look with its dark red paintwork and sash windows but through the windows they could see well stocked shelves of just about everything you could want to decorate and furnish a home.

"Come on," said Jessica, "I love this place. I used to come here when I was younger and imagine I was decorating my own home. I'd spend ages choosing the colours and cushions and rugs. Wow," she said, pointing across to the bedroom furniture, "see that white wardrobe, I love that style. Traditional but with a youthfulness about it," she said, laughing.

"Are you practising to be a TV presenter," said Marie laughing with her.

"Maybe," said Jessica. She grinned.

"Well I think you're a natural," said Marie, "very flamboyant."

"Come on you two, the paints are over here," said Ellie leading them across the store. "What colours do you like?"

"I'm not sure," said Jessica wandering across to the wallpapers. She picked up a number of floral prints, "I really like this," she said holding up a paper covered in bluebells. "It reminds me of our walks through the woods. I know it's a quick decision but this is definitely the one."

"I wish I was as decisive as you," said Marie. "Just the paint to go then. Cream or blue, or were you thinking something totally different, like orange?"

"Blue," she replied, "a warm light blue. This one," she said holding up a pot of paint.

"I think it's perfect," said Ellie. "I'll have to get you to help choose colours for the cottage."

"Come on," said Jessica, "I need to get back and help Edward."

"No you don't," said Marie as she paid, "that's what I'm here for. Straight home and put your feet up, we've a busy day tomorrow."

6

Jessica had been banished from upstairs so she sat in the tea room eating her breakfast. Edward had made granary toast topped with mashed avocado and poached eggs, he was becoming quite accomplished in the kitchen. She could hear a lot of movement and every now and again Edward would disappear to move something. If she needed to rest she had to tell Edward and be escorted to her room and then text when she wanted to leave. She would have liked to try baking some more bread but Pat and Edward were busy in the kitchen preparing for lunch.

"You look a bit fed up," said Pat.

"I feel a bit useless. Mum and Marie are busy upstairs, Edward's running about and I'm just smiling at customers," Jessica said.

"Come on, it's a bit quieter at the moment, I'll show you how to make one of the cakes," said Pat.

Jessica wasn't that keen on baking cakes, she used to help her mum out from time to time but it was never something she thought she'd do herself. However, she thought she ought to learn, after all she was going to continue offering cakes in the tea room and Edward couldn't do it all.

"I was about to make a lemon cake as we are running low, I'll get the ingredients out of the cupboard and you can weigh and add everything to the mixer, whisk it up and then bake. We can make the drizzle mixture whilst it's cooking," Pat said as she turned on the oven. "We tend to make most of the cakes in the square tins as they are easier to cut but you might want to change this, Edward was telling me you wanted to try out some new ideas."

"Square is fine," Jessica said, she tried to sound enthusiastic but she really wanted to learn how to make bread not cakes.

Pat called out the ingredients and weights, she held most of the recipes in her head, whilst Jessica weighed and added everything to the mixer. As she turned the mixer on Edward came into the kitchen. "I think I ought to write these down. I'll have to start a recipe file on my laptop," he said.

"You are so organised," said Jessica throwing a tea towel at him.

"Not really, just forgetful," he said laughing and throwing the tea towel back.

Jessica whisked up the mixture and poured it into the two square tins which she'd lined with greaseproof paper. She popped them in the oven and set the timer for forty-five minutes.

"Drizzle next," said Pat.

Jessica's face must have shown her lack of enthusiasm because Edward spoke up.

"Can I have a go?" he said. "And I think you should sit down for a while. The tea room is fairly quiet, sit at a table and I'll bring you a coffee."

"Thank-you," said Jessica, "and don't forget to write it down so I can give it a go later," she said winking at Edward.

As Edward brought put her coffee on the table the doorbell jangled.

"Delivery," said a man as he walked in.

Edward ran to meet him. "Round the back," he said.

"What's going on," Jessica asked.

"Don't you worry, have your coffee, I'll be back in a minute," he said following the delivery man out of the tea room.

Jessica sat down and sipped her coffee. She hated not knowing what was going on, she liked to be part of things.

By the end of the day Jessica felt tired, she'd taken a break and gone to her room to lie down but the noise coming from Mum's room, mainly giggling, had kept her awake so she'd decided she may as well help out downstairs. Once the last customer had left she kicked off her shoes. The doorbell jangled.

"We've just closed," said Jessica as a man walked into the tea room.

"Don't worry, I've come to collect the furniture," he said.

"What furniture?" Jessica asked.

"I've got this," said Edward as he came rushing out of the kitchen, "it's all under control."

Edward led the man towards the hall. "You can lock up we'll go out the back," he said.

"I thought this was going to be a lick of paint," Jessica said. "From the amount of coming and going it seems like you've gutted the whole upstairs."

"Maybe we have, but you'll just have to wait and see," Edward said. "Not much longer now."

As much as she loved surprises Jessica hated waiting. Edward had left her a plate of sandwiches but these weren't going to occupy her for long. If she wasn't so tired she'd start pacing. The suspense was killing her, she needed to distract herself somehow.

"Surprise," said Edward as he came back into the tea room.

"Is it ready, can I see it?" Jessica asked.

"Not yet, but I've got you this," he said holding out a bag.

"What is it?" asked Jessica.

"Look inside," Edward said.

Jessica took the bag, she pulled out a book of bread recipes, full colour with lots of pictures, and a DVD with videos.

"Wow," she said as she flicked through the pages, she would have hugged him but standing up was too much effort right now. "I've already spotted a recipe for olive bread."

"I thought it would keep you occupied until they're finished," he said.

"Does it look good?" she asked.

"I don't know," he said. "All I've done is help carry a few bits upstairs. I'm sure it'll be lovely though, after all I believe you chose the colours." He bent down and kissed her. "I've just got to clear up the kitchen then we'll wait together."

It was another hour before Marie and Ellie came down into the tea room.

"Come on up," they said together.

Jessica stood up, she would have run up the stairs but that might be a bit ambitious at the moment, so a slow walk it was.

"Time for the big reveal," Marie said. "Do you remember what it looked like this morning?"

"Careful how you answer that," said Ellie laughing.

"To be honest I haven't been in there since we moved in so no I don't remember," said Jessica.

"Close your eyes, both of you," Marie said standing in front of the bedroom door.

Jessica closed he eyes and shuffled into the room, she felt Edward beside her, he held her hand.

"One, two, three, open," shouted Marie.

Jessica opened her eyes. "Wow," she said.

"Wow," said Edward.

Jessica looked around the room trying to take it all in. The wallpaper she had chosen was on the wall behind the bed and there was new matching bedlinen and blue curtains, the same bluebell blue as the wallpaper.

"It's a new bed," she said noting the white painted headboard.

"It is," said Ellie, "we knew you'd decided not to bring your old one from Bristol so we thought you might like this."

"And the wardrobes, and drawers," Jessica said as she looked around. "They're the ones we saw yesterday. How did you get them delivered today?"

"As if by fate they had the display furniture on sale. I persuaded them to deliver today," Ellie said. "You can move it around if you don't like the layout."

"I love it. Edward did you know?" asked Jessica.

"I knew furniture was arriving but I didn't realise how good it would look," he said gripping her hand.

Jessica curled her toes and felt them sink into the soft carpet. "A new carpet," she said looking down, "I'm never going to leave this room."

"Well I was hoping you might still do the odd shift in the tea room," Edward said raising his eyebrows.

"We've one more surprise," said Ellie, "close your eyes again and step a bit further into the room."

Jessica and Edward stepped into the room and Ellie shut the door behind them.

"Turn around and open," Ellie said.

Jessica turned around and opened her eyes. There was a beautiful white painted cot made up with lemon and white bedding. There was a small teddy bear in the corner. She couldn't speak. She felt the tears fill her eyes.

Edward squeezed her hand. "Thank-you," he said looking at Marie and Ellie. "It's beautiful. Perfect."

Jessica wiped her cheeks. "Thank-you," she said. "I can't quite believe it. It feels like our home, mine, Edward's and this little one." She patted her bump.

7

The smell of freshly brewed coffee wafted into the bedroom. Jessica opened her eyes. She still couldn't believe how her mum and sister had managed to transform the room into this amazing bedroom in just one day. She sat up and switched on the lamp, the new curtains had blackout lining ready for when the baby arrived. There was a mirror opposite the bed so she could see the reflection of the bluebell wallpaper. It reminded her of late spring, those few weeks that promised summer wasn't too far away.

"Morning," said Edward as he brought a cup of coffee to Jessica and put it on the new bedside table. "How are you feeling?"

"Great," she said, and she meant it. Maybe she had finally caught up with the lost sleep after the house move. "Do you think we can have another go at bread making?" she said. "I've made loads of notes and I think I know where I went wrong."

"Are you sure you're up to it?" he said.

"Stop fussing, I feel fine," she answered sipping her coffee.

Edward drew back the curtains a little. "It's pretty grim out there," he said, "I think we could be quiet. We'll have to get everything ready for the tea room and then yes we'll commandeer the kitchen."

There was a knock on the open bedroom door.

"Morning," said Marie, "I'll help you set up the tea room if you like. Mum's out with Michael so I'm at your disposal."

"Excellent," said Jessica, "I'm glad it's working out with Mum and Michael, she deserves it, it's been a long time since Dad died."

Marie smiled and nodded at her.

"I'll be up very soon," Jessica said. "If we all get the tea room ready we can make bread this morning. We don't need any more cakes so I'm sure we can work around Pat if we get customers."

"Well I hope we get some customers, but yes, if we get going now I'm sure we can give it a go before the lunchtime rush," said Edward.

"I've got a list of ideas," said Jessica easing her legs out of bed, "that book was great."

"Let's start with something basic and then we can work on your list," said Edward helping his wife to stand up.

As soon as she had eaten breakfast, Edward always insisted she didn't do anything until she had eaten, Jessica went down to help set up the tea room, this was probably the earliest they'd started work.

"Marie, I'm so glad you're here," said Jessica as they changed the tablecloths together. "How long can you stay?"

"Only a day or two more," Marie said, "I've got to get back to work. But I will be back when you have the baby, I'm not missing out on being a proper auntie."

Jessica unlocked the tea room door, "I can't believe how dark it's getting, I think we'll be in for some rain later," she said.

"Well if it's quiet you and Edward can get on with your bread, and even if it's busy I'm sure we can manage," said Marie.

Edward walked into the tea room. "All done in the kitchen," he said, "I'm ready when you are."

Pat came out of the kitchen, "I've moved as much as I can out of your way," she said.

"Thanks Pat," Jessica said, "we should only be a couple of hours." As she glanced out of the window she noticed that a few people were opening umbrellas or pulling up hoods. It was still quite warm but it looked like this was the end of the Indian summer.

"Let's see what we can do," said Edward. He took the flour out of the cupboard. "I've bought extra flour and some dried yeast as I wasn't sure when we'd next get a chance to have a go."

Jessica opened her book. "I'll read out the recipe and you

can weigh," she said.

An hour and a half later they had three batches of bread rising in the kitchen. One farmhouse white, one wholemeal and one olive. Edward had surprised her with a tub of olives, "just so you can give it a try," he'd said.

This time Edward had done all the first kneading by hand.

"Ready for second kneading?" Edward said.

Jessica tipped the first batch of white dough onto the floured worktop. "I'll give this one a go," she said, "but you might need to finish it off."

Another hour and all the bread was shaped and on trays, after a second rising it could be baked.

Jessica switched on the ovens.

Marie walked in. "How's it going?" she asked.

"Great, I think," said Jessica. "It can go into the oven soon." She took a peek under one of the cloths. "It looks okay."

"Of course it's okay," said Edward, "we make an awesome team."

"Well it's fairly quiet out there," Marie said, "I think everyone's getting their shopping done and going home."

"I'll get these in the oven and then give you a break," said Jessica.

Jessica put the bread in the oven and set the timer, she also set a manual timer to put in the tea room, just in case she didn't hear the oven timers.

As Jessica went into the tea room the doorbell jangled and two customers walked in, they closed their umbrellas and put them in the wooden stand. Jessica glanced out of the window the rain was getting heavier, she could hear the tapping sound it made as it fell onto the tables outside.

As she led the customers to a table the rain started to hammer against the windows. Within moments Jessica could see rivulets of water running down the side of the road. People started to rush into the tea room to escape the downpour. Jessica and Marie tried to seat everyone before taking orders for hot drinks.

Jessica carried out a tray of hot chocolate and a plate of cakes; there was a flash of lightening followed by a crash of thunder. Jessica froze, her heart started to race, she had always been afraid of thunder. Right now she wanted to go upstairs and hide under her duvet.

Marie turned on the overhead lights and lamps on the sideboard; it had suddenly gone very dark. "You alright?" asked Marie as a second crash of thunder caused the windows to vibrate.

"I will be, I'm sure it'll soon pass," Jessica said trying to smile.

Jessica jumped again as lightening lit up the tea room, simultaneously there was a loud bang; the lights flashed and the tea room went dark.

The emergency lighting came on automatically. Jessica tried a few of the light switches but there was definitely no power. She looked out of the window and saw that the neighbouring shops were also in semi-darkness. The rain was still hammering down; the water now ran right across the road; it was beginning to look like a fast running river. The street was empty of people. A sudden gust of wind caught one of the outside tables and sent it into the road.

"Edward quick," Jessica said.

One of the customers rushed out with Edward to bring in the tables and chairs, each time they opened the door the rain drove in.

"What shall we do," asked Jessica when Edward came back in.

"Well I'll have to change first," he said as a puddle of rain water started to form at his feet. "I'm literally soaked through."

Jessica stood in the middle of the tea room, it was very noisy, not least because of the rain and thunder. "Can I have your attention," she said. "We can't take any orders at the moment and the coffee machine is out but we do have plenty of hot water in the urn. If you can bear with us we'll make pots of tea and give everyone a cup."

A cheer went up.

Jessica set about making pots of tea and putting them on the counter, Marie and Pat poured them into cups and handed them out to customers. They put milk and sugar on all the tables and a few extra on the counter for those customers who were standing. They cut small slices of cakes and piled them onto plates, Marie carried them around the tea room offering them to everyone.

Edward walked back into the tea room, he had changed into dry clothes although his hair was still wet.

"Looks like you have things under control," he said, raising an eyebrow at Jessica.

The buzzer went off on the counter.

"Oh no, the bread," said Jessica, "it'll be ruined."

"I'll get it," said Edward.

A few minutes later he came out of the kitchen with plates of warm bread cut into small pieces. "It's actually quite good," he said.

Jessica took a piece, "It is, how come?" she said.

"I guess the ovens stayed just hot enough to finish cooking them." Edward said.

Edward handed the bread to the customers.

"This is good," said a lady near to the counter, she still had her coat on. "What is it?"

"That's the olive bread," said Jessica.

Ten minutes later the rain started to ease and the power came back on. The customers started to leave thanking Jessica for her hospitality.

The lady in the coat turned to Jessica, "I've never been in here before," she said, "but if that bread is anything to go by I'll definitely be coming here for lunch next time I come to town."

Edward smiled at Jessica. "I think we could be onto something here," he said as he picked up another piece of bread.

8

Sunday morning was showing all the signs of being a warm and sunny day. After the storm of yesterday Jessica had thought that Autumn had arrived with a vengeance but maybe it would hold off just a little longer, even the roads had dried. She changed the cloth on the table nearest the window, it was early but already a few people were walking around the town, she noticed a young woman with a small boy, she assumed it was her son. They were both holding the lead of a large black dog who looked quite content to be out for his morning walk. Jessica looked down at her bump, maybe this little one would like a pet, perhaps a hamster or a fish, they might even be able to manage a small dog. She'd have to talk to Edward about it.

Jessica walked through the tea room and turned on the coffee machine before going into the kitchen. "Morning," she said watching Edward as he cooked breakfast.

"Morning," he replied, "two eggs coming up."

"You don't have to cook me breakfast every morning you know," she said.

"Oh yes I do else it would be lunchtime before you ate," he said.

"You're probably right," she said smiling. "What were you up to last night? I heard you in the kitchen but I didn't hear you come to bed."

"Sorry, I was working on the plans for your bakery," he said.

"Our bakery," she said, correcting him.

"Our bakery," he said as he put the eggs onto the toast. "Sunny side up, just the way you like them."

"That's excellent," she said putting an arm around him.

"It's only eggs," he said.

"No, about the plans," she said punching him on the arm. "When can we start?"

"Have your breakfast then we'll talk," he replied carrying her plate into the tea room.

"Edward, you sound like something's wrong," she said following him out of the kitchen.

"Not exactly, I'm sure we can make it work but it might take a little time," he said.

"That's okay, a week or two won't hurt, as long as we are up and running before the baby arrives," she said.

Edward sat down with her. "Unless this little one plans on taking another month or two we won't be ready," he said. "We might have to wait a while before we become master bakers."

Jessica put her fork down. "We had a quick look yesterday evening," she said, "we can get an extra oven and even take delivery in a few days."

"You're right, but I had a long look," he said as he reached across the table and took her hand. "We need a bit more equipment than just the oven, at least if we are going to do this properly."

"Are you saying we can't afford it," she said.

"No, I'm not saying that," he said still holding her hand, "although we will have to go through the figures again. But we can't just plug this stuff in - we need to get it installed by a professional."

"That shouldn't be too hard," Jessica said, feeling a little relieved, this was a problem she could definitely solve. "There must be someone local, Mum is sure to have contacts. It shouldn't hold us up."

"Maybe not but what will hold us up is that we don't have enough room," he said, letting go of her hand as she pulled it away.

"Of course we have the room - we can take a unit out of the kitchen," she said picking up the edge of her napkin and twisting it in her hands.

"It won't be enough, we need more space for all the kit and to work in. There is no way we can bake bread and also make the cakes and sandwiches we need for the day. We'd have to stay up all night," he said.

"There's got to be a way. I'm not giving up that easy,"

she said.

"No-one said you have to give up, we just need to give it some thought and accept it will take a little while," he said. "I'm sure you want to get this right."

"I hope this isn't your way of putting me off," she said still twisting her napkin.

"No, you can look at my notes if you like," he said sounding frustrated, "we've got some options, we could build an extension or convert the downstairs room. Either way we'll likely need planning permission and that will take time as well as more money. Now eat your eggs."

Jessica pushed how plate to one side. "I'm not very hungry," she said.

"You have to eat," he said.

"I know but I'm really not hungry," she replied. "I'll set up the tea room and then eat, you can watch me if you like."

"Don't look so down about this, it isn't even a setback, we just need to make some decisions about how to take this forward," he said.

"You wouldn't understand," she said getting up. She held onto the table for a few seconds as she felt a twinge in her back. She noticed Edward's look of concern. "And I'm fine so stop worrying."

"I do understand, as you said this is our bakery. I want this to work as much as you," he said.

"You'd be happy if we kept things as they are," she said frowning at him.

"For a short time yes. But I do want to make this our own - for the three of us," he said as he picked up her plate.

The doorbell jangled and Pat walked in.

"You're both looking very serious," she said.

"Just trying to get Jessica to eat her breakfast," Edward said.

Marie walked into the tea room.

"Here to help," she said brightly.

"Perfect timing," Jessica said trying to smile.

****

The rest of the day was busy with a steady stream of customers coming for morning coffee or afternoon tea. By the end of the day Jessica felt particularly uncomfortable and, even though she hated to admit it, exhausted. She had wanted to talk to Edward but decided to get an early night, they could go through the plans tomorrow. For the first time in a long while she decided to go to bed early. She slept straight through until the following morning.

9

After a such a good sleep Jessica enjoyed working in the tea room. It was a little quieter than the weekend which meant she had time to chat to Marie before she left for London. Edward had been quiet all day and had popped out a couple of times, he'd said he had to get supplies but he seemed deep in thought, almost sullen. Jessica guessed he was annoyed with her for not talking to him about his plans.

At the end of the day Jessica said good-bye to the last customers as they walked out of the tea room into the sunshine, another t-shirt and sandals day. Her feet ached so she kicked off her shoes, there was no way she was going to bend down and pick them up. The burst of energy she'd had this morning had left her and the twinges were back. She was beginning to think she'd have to really slow down for the next two weeks.

Marie came out of the kitchen. "You should sit down," she said, "take the weight off your feet."

"Nearly finished," Jessica said picking up a tray.

"Oh," she said putting the tray back on the table. She put her hands on her stomach. "This one's certainly active today."

She went to pick the tray up again and winced.

"Are you okay?" asked Marie. "Sit down, I'll clear up."

Jessica held on to the back of the chair and took a deep breath, "I don't think sitting down will help," she said.

"You don't mean…," said Marie, "I'll get Edward, I'll call Mum," she said her voice rising a little.

"What's all the commotion about," said Edward coming out of the kitchen.

"It's the baby," said Marie.

"But we've got another two weeks," said Edward as he helped Jessica onto a chair.

"I don't think so," said Marie. "You need to call the hospital, get Jessica's bag and bring the car around."

"I'm sure we've got plenty of time," said Jessica in

between taking a few deep breaths, "the midwife told us to…." She stopped speaking as she felt another contraction.

"Well I'm not waiting," said Edward, "we are going right now," he paused, "just in case," he said calmly.

Pat came out of the kitchen. "Come on," she said, "I'll clear up but don't forget to call me."

"Where's your bag Jessica?" asked Marie.

"I haven't packed it yet, I thought I had plenty of time," she said. She looked at Edward. "I think we need to go now."

"Don't worry I'll put some things together and bring it along. Edward go and get the car," Marie said.

Edward ran up the stairs to get the keys, a few minutes later he had pulled the car near the front of the tea room. Marie held on to Jessica's arm and helped her out of the door and along the path. A few passersby looked concerned and offered to help.

"Don't worry," Marie said indicating up the road with a nod. "The car's just up there." She held on tight to Jessica.

"I'm not sure I can make it," Jessica said

"Just a few more steps, look Edward has the door open already, I'll follow right behind," Marie said her voice sounding a little shaky.

"Have you called Mum," Jessica asked.

"I've asked Pat to ring her, I'll check when I get back in," Marie said. "I'll go and pack you a bag and bring it to the hospital."

"Be quick, and find Mum," Jessica said as Edward helped her into the car. She sat down, took a deep breath and held it as another contraction took hold. "I'm not sure I'm going to make it," she said turning to Edward.

"Just try and stay calm. I've rung the hospital and they're expecting you," he said pulling into the traffic.

Edward pulled in front of the hospital doors. Jessica started to sweat, she began to feel scared.

"You'll be fine, we're in the right place. I'll get you inside and then move the car," Edward said smiling at her.

"Don't leave me," she said.

"I'll only be a few minutes, and you won't be alone," he said.

Within minutes Jessica was in a delivery room, her midwife had already examined her and asked her questions about pain relief. Edward was back by her side.

"The midwife said we were right to come in straight away," Edward said. "She'll be in and out, keeping an eye on you, but says not to worry, it's all going well."

"Where's Mum?" asked Jessica with an edge of panic in her voice. "I need her here."

"I'm sure she's on her way, Marie's outside and is trying to reach her," said Edward reassuringly.

"What if she doesn't get here, she wasn't coming back until late, she might not even have left yet," said Jessica her voice rising.

"I'm here," said Edward, "and I'm not going anywhere."

A couple of hours after she had arrived at the hospital the midwife examined her again. "You've not long to go now," she said.

"This baby is not being born until my mum gets here," said Jessica firmly.

"I'm afraid you may not have a choice," said the midwife, "don't worry we'll take good care of you."

Jessica took another deep breath and tears started to prick her eyes.

"Jessica, how are you doing," said a voice as the door opened.

"Mum," cried Jessica.

"Are you ready now?" asked the midwife smiling.

"Like you said," said Jessica taking another deep breath, "I don't think I have a choice." She grabbed the hands of Edward and her mum.

Time stopped for Jessica, it could have been minutes or hours, she was aware of being given instructions and also the reassuring voices of her mum and Edward. Eventually she gave a final push.

"Well done," said the midwife, "you have a beautiful

boy."

Jessica sat up a little and held her newborn baby boy in her arms, the tears now ran freely down her face.

"Can you text Marie," Jessica said looking at Edward. "She must have been waiting outside for ages."

"Already have," said Edward, "she's on her way."

Marie walked in carrying a brown paper bag.

"My first nephew," said Marie hugging her sister. "You're so clever."

"What's in the bag?" asked Jessica. "You can't have been to the shops already."

"Edward asked me to bring it in from your car," she said as she handed the bag to Edward.

Edward opened the bag and took out a bread roll. "I know this isn't the best time to discuss the tea room but try this," he said. He broke off a small piece and popped it into Jessica's mouth.

"This is great," she said, "just what I was hoping for, did you make it?"

"Not exactly," Edward replied.

"You didn't buy it?" she asked.

"Not exactly," he said again.

"Come on Edward, I'm tired, what's going on," Jessica said.

"I know how important this is to you so I went and had a chat at the local bakery. They said they'd be happy to work with you to make the type of breads that you want. And they can supply daily," said Edward smiling.

"That sounds perfect," said Jessica. She looked down at the baby. "Especially as I think we might be a little busy for the next few weeks."

Ellie gently took the baby from Jessica. "Have you got a shortlist of names?" she asked.

"We had a long list of names for a girl but we only had one name for a boy," said Edward looking at Jessica and smiling as he squeezed her hand. "James."

"After Dad," said Jessica.

Ellie started to cry. "I think that's wonderful," she said between the tears. She looked down at the baby. "Welcome to the family James."

The End

Book Three

The Vintage Tea Room 3
changing times and new opportunities

Lily Wells

1

Marie shifted in the back seat of the taxi, it had been a long journey from London and she was feeling stiff. There had been a problem with the train and all passengers had to take a coach from Reading, she was now two hours later than expected. At least the taxi had air conditioning; she welcomed this early summer but being on the road in the heat was no fun.

She glanced out of the window and smiled as the familiar sites of her old home town came into view. The honey coloured buildings, the tall stone walls surrounding the parkland and the narrow medieval streets with quirky shops and cafes. Several years had passed since she'd moved away and yet it still felt like coming home.

"We're here," said the taxi driver as he pulled over to the side of the road. He opened his door and walked to the back of the car. "You been to Cirencester before?" he asked.

"Yes," she said smiling. "I know it quite well."

"Well if you need to go anywhere give me a call," he said as he took Marie's suitcase from the boot of the car.

"Thanks," said Marie. She stepped out, stood for a moment as she adjusted to the heat, and handed him the fare.

It had been six months since she'd last visited. She looked towards the tea room, today the street was bathed in the afternoon sunshine, the sun was still high in the sky as the longest day approached. This was a bit different from the last time she'd visited when she'd been faced with what could only be described as a blizzard. Even then the town had looked welcoming, the snow on the pavements was challenging and she'd nearly slipped more than once, but it made the winter feel like, well, winter.

This time was more than just a flying visit. It had come as quite a surprise when her mum had called to say she was getting married. Marie had been so caught up in her work that she hadn't noticed the two years that had gone by since her mum had first met Michael. She'd been about to tell her that they should wait, that this seemed like a whirlwind romance, but then she'd glanced at a photo of her nephew and realised that James hadn't even been born when her mum had gone on that first date with her fiancé.

Marie walked slowly towards the tea room pulling her suitcase behind. A few of the shops were open, many closed on Sundays, the smell of ground coffee drifted from one of the cafes, it reminded her of London except here the pleasant aroma was not mixed with the smell of diesel fumes.

As she glanced in a shop window she caught sight of her reflection, automatically she put her hand up to her hair. Edgy, her hairdresser had called it. The short angular cut that was supposed to make her look professional, current and on-trend. It obviously had the desired effect because she'd been offered the promotion. She needed to ring her boss this week and formally accept.

She stopped when she reached the tea room and peered through the window, it was empty, it had probably been closed for at least half an hour. Jessica and Edward had continued to put their own stamp on the place since buying it from Mum but they'd left a few things unchanged. Marie noticed there were photographs and paintings hanging on the walls, each had a small price tag underneath. Mum had always supported local artists and it seemed Jessica enjoyed this too.

When Marie pushed against the door the bell gave its familiar jingle. She looked around hoping to see Jessica and James. Last time she was here her nephew had been taking his first tentative steps. Thanks to video calling she knew he was now trying to run everywhere, usually with a few stumbles along the way.

"We're closed," a male voice came from the kitchen.

Marie didn't recognise the voice, it wasn't Edward.

"It's Marie," she called back.

"We're still closed," the man said as he came out of the kitchen drying his hands with a tea towel. "We open at nine tomorrow."

"I know but," she paused. She was quite surprised by his manner, whoever he was. If she was a customer she probably wouldn't come back in the morning. The man scowled at her and returned to the kitchen.

"Marie," Jessica said as she almost ran from the hall into the tea room. She hugged her sister tightly. "I'm so glad you're here. Mum's really stressed about the wedding and Pat's on holiday and we're so busy at the moment." Jessica stopped suddenly and stepped back. "Wow," she said. "Your hair is fantastic. Quite a change." She hugged her sister again and grabbed her suitcase.

"Thanks, thought I'd try something different," said Marie. "Who's the guy." She nodded towards the kitchen.

"You've met Adam then," said Jessica as she pushed against the door into the hall.

"He's a little offhand isn't he?" Marie said following her sister up the stairs.

"He's great, a really good cook," said Jessica. "We're so lucky to have him even if it is only for the short term."

"Well I guess you know him better than me," Marie said. She wasn't convinced that Jessica knew how he behaved when he was out of her earshot. "Combining motherhood with being an entrepreneur really suits you, you look great too."

"I don't know about that," said Jessica grinning. "Sometimes I go to bed wondering how I ever made it to the end of the day. Coffee?"

"Yes please," said Marie. "And where's this young nephew of mine. I can't wait to see him."

"He's out with Edward," said Jessica as she filled the kettle. "He's been so excited Edward had to take him to the park just to wear him out a bit."

"That's quite handy actually," said Marie. "I wanted to have a chat with you."

"Sounds ominous," said Jessica.

"No, it's just that…," Marie said. "Seems like it'll have to wait." Marie grinned and turned towards the door as she heard the sound of tiny feet scrambling up the stairs.

James came running, or rather stumbling, towards her.

"Hug, hug," he said with his arms outstretched.

"His latest word," said Jessica smiling at Marie.

James tripped as he leaned towards Marie. She put out her arms and caught him, sweeping him up into the air.

"You have grown so much," said Marie hugging James. "I can't believe you're running around so well. Last time I was here you could barely walk."

James put his arms around Marie's neck. "Kiss, kiss," he said.

Marie obligingly planted a kiss on the top of his head.

"I think he's missed you," said Edward as he made himself a cup of coffee.

"I've missed him," said Marie. "All of you in fact." She ruffled James' hair.

"You wanted to chat," said Jessica. "We can go into the sitting room if you like."

"It can wait," said Marie. "I think James would like play."

She put James on the floor and held his hand. He led her into his bedroom in search of a favourite toy.

Marie spent the rest of the evening playing with James. Jessica was right, he had endless energy and was quite reluctant to go to bed. "One more," was becoming quite a catchphrase as she pushed cars around his small race track and read him stories. By the time he was settled Marie was ready for bed herself.

"I'll see you in the morning," Marie said smiling at Jessica as she picked up her mug of hot chocolate. "We can chat then."

2

Marie opened her eyes as the warmth of the sun crept through the gap in the curtains. Just a moment more, she thought to herself. A few more minutes of enjoying the feeling of being totally relaxed before she was given a list of jobs to do by Jessica or her mum. The room was the same as it had been the day she moved out. Jessica had moved into Mum's old room and redecorated her own bedroom for James, but this room, her old room, had been left untouched. The curtains, the furniture, even the quilt, were the same. It made her feel at home, even if it had been a long time since she'd lived here.

"Morning," said Jessica walking in carrying a mug of steaming coffee.

"Morning," said Marie. "Room service, I could get used to this." She cleared a space on the bedside table.

"I wouldn't, you know what I'm like," said Jessica grinning. "It could be days before I remembered you were waiting for me. Mum's meeting us at the arboretum so I thought I'd better make an early start. She can't wait to catch up with you and go through the wedding plans. For some reason she seems to think you're a better organiser than me." She frowned but she couldn't stop the corners of her mouth from turning slightly up. "Of course, she's probably right." She grinned.

"You're being unfair on yourself," Marie said. "You seem to manage all of this pretty well."

"Only because I have help." Jessica said. "Anyway, I've got to sort out the tea room, we need to leave in less than an hour."

Jessica got out of bed and headed for the shower. She could drink her coffee whilst she got ready. Hopefully she'd have a chance to talk to Jessica later in the day.

Within the hour she sat in the car with Jessica heading towards Westonbirt. James was strapped into his car seat in the back. He was quite happy chattering away to himself. Every now and again Marie could make out a word such as car or nana. He was a happy boy who laughed a lot and was clearly enjoying the car journey.

The road towards Tetbury was a familiar one, they'd driven along it many times when she was a child. She looked out the window at the low stone walls protecting the inhabitants of the fields, and the small areas of woodland that provided shelter for wildlife. As she watched two deer ran into a field pausing briefly to look around before continuing across towards the trees. They drove passed a pair of cottages with gardens full of vegetables and flowers. One garden had a homemade scarecrow proudly looking towards the road. Marie was about to point it out to James but they had driven by before she had the chance.

Finally, they came to the outskirts of Tetbury. This had changed quite considerably over the years with a new supermarket and a lot of new houses. The centre of the small market town, though, had changed little. It still had its multitude of antique shops and cafes. Some of the banks had become boutiques and some of the shops fronts had a modern look but mostly the buildings looked as they had for centuries. Many of the shops had been here since Marie was a child, the cheese shop on Church Street had a fantastic selection of cheeses, pates and chutneys – she shopped here whenever she visited the town. The violin maker on Long Street was still there, although she'd never had cause to visit this particular shop. And the Market Hall still stood on its pillars overlooking the centre of town; today there must be market or exhibition inside as people were walking up and down the stone steps at the front. As they drove by Marie admired the huge hanging baskets full of colour. Someone must have been watering them as rain like droplets fell onto the pavements below and almost instantly evaporated in the heat.

The town soon gave way to the countryside. The pavements became grass verges and the houses became interspersed with fields. A small herd of black and white cows looked quite content grazing in the sunshine.

James pointed out of the window. "Moo," he said.

"Moo," replied Marie. She turned to him and laughed.

When she'd lived here she'd taken all of this for granted. There were green spaces in London, and some large parks. Police rode horses through the city but there were few cows, or sheep or meadows full of wild flowers. She really appreciated seeing it now.

A few minutes later they turned onto the long drive leading to the arboretum's car park. To the right were the paddocks that were used as additional parking when the place was busy. She'd been here on days when even these overflow car parks were full. Today they were able to park near the Welcome Building.

James started to wriggle in his seat. "Nana, nana," he shouted as Ellie walked towards their car.

Marie jumped out of the car and hugged her mum. "How are you?" she asked. "Jessica says you're worrying about the wedding."

Ellie looked at Jessica and shook her head. "I'm fine," she said, "everything's organised." She smiled. "It's Jessica who's worrying, she just wants everything to be perfect. As I keep telling her, it already is."

"Well let me know what I can do," said Marie.

"I will," said Ellie. "I have to say your hair looks stunning, a real city look. Did you get it cut for the wedding?"

"Thanks, and yes," said Marie. This was a little white lie but she could tell her mum about the job after the weekend.

It took more than a few minutes to get the pushchair out of the car, James strapped in and his bag full of essentials safely tucked away.

"I can't believe one small boy can need so much stuff," said Marie picking up his toy airplane from the back seat.

"Well there's the snacks, toys, wipes…," Jessica said sighing.

James wriggled in his pushchair and held his arms out to be picked up.

"He can run around once we're inside," Jessica said.

"So how's my favourite grandson?" said Ellie as she took the pushchair from Jessica.

"He's fine," said Jessica. "A bit over excited seeing both you and his Auntie Marie."

"I don't think James is going to sit still for long," said Ellie as she watched him trying to manoeuvre his arm out of the strap. "Let's walk before having a coffee."

They scanned their annual passes and walked through the gates. Even though Marie only visited once or twice a year she still felt it worth the small fee as this was one place they could all come together and catch up whilst James ran around. She still enjoyed walking amongst the trees noting the changes across the seasons. Today the trees were in full leaf. She often marvelled at the range of colours - greens, golden yellows and the reds of the acers. Even the shades of green were different, some light, others dark, some with a hint of blue. Marie stopped and took a photograph on her phone, she liked to capture the moments she spent with her family.

"Where first?" asked Marie. "It's a while since I've been here."

"The Treetop Walk," said Jessica. "James loves it."

They followed the path to the left, Marie stopped when a brown and white spaniel ran up to her. She patted him on the head. He immediately ran back across the grass and picked up a ball his owner had thrown for him.

"This is new," said Marie. She stopped at the edge of the Treetop Walk. The wooden and steel structure headed skywards.

"Yes," said Jessica. "James likes to try and run across and I have to try and keep up."

Jessica lifted James out of his pushchair, Ellie held his hand as he tried to run ahead. As they started the gentle ascent up the wooden walkway James kept looking down between the boards. He seemed fascinated with how high up they were going. Ellie pointed out a few of the trees to James – beech, oak, hazel. James pointed and tried to copy the words but ended up calling everything a tree, at least it sounded a little like tree. Ellie laughed. Marie thought back to the times Mum had brought her and Jessica here and had tried to teach them the differences between the species, she couldn't remember how many she used to recognise but now her knowledge was limited.

"This is his favourite bit," said Jessica. James was stood on a glass panel looking down to the ground below. He started to jump up and down.

"James," said Marie. "Be careful."

"Don't say that," said Jessica. "He'll jump even harder."

Marie laughed as she watched James running backwards and forwards across the panel before running ahead with Ellie following close behind.

"It's the small suspension bridge next," Jessica said. "Another opportunity to jump and scare me."

Marie smiled as her mum and nephew ran ahead. By the time they'd caught up James and Ellie had run across the bridge, around the wooden platform and were back on the main walkway.

"That's high," said Marie looking up to the crow's nest. "Surely James can't go up there?"

"He would if he could but no, we don't let him yet," said Jessica.

Ellie had already picked up James and was leading him away from temptation.

"You two go on up," said Ellie. "I'll meet you at the end."

"Are you going up?" said Jessica.

"I don't know," said Marie. "Is it safe?"

"Come on," said Jessica. She started to climb the steps. "It's a little steep so I can't carry James up here, the platform moves when you're up there but the view's great."

Marie put one foot tentatively onto the step. She held onto the side. It wasn't quite a ladder but it was steeper than a staircase. When she reached the top she moved quickly to the side and hung onto the rail.

"Whoa," she said. "You really can feel it move."

She looked over the side. She waved to James who was pointing upwards and bouncing in Ellie's arms. Jessica was going to have to hang onto him when he got bigger.

"So, are you going to tell me what's bothering you?" asked Jessica as she stood beside her sister.

"Nothing's actually bothering me but I would like to talk to you," Marie said. "Not here though. Let's head back down, the views are great but I'm sure I'm feeling a little motion sickness."

"And I always thought you weren't afraid of anything," Jessica said laughing. "I've always looked up to my big sister."

"We're twins," said Marie heading down the steps. "And I'm not afraid, it's just the movement."

"You're still the eldest," said Jessica following her down.

"We were minutes apart," said Marie as she put both feet back onto the solid walkway.

Jessica grabbed the pushchair and followed Marie as they caught up with Ellie and James.

"Are you really ready for the weekend?" asked Marie looking at her mum. "I was hoping to have something to do."

"You need to get the final fitting on your dresses and then pick up the outfits for Grace and James." Ellie said. "I've no idea if James will walk quietly behind me, I've a sneaky feeling he might just try to steal the show." She laughed and ruffled his hair.

"All organised," said Marie. "We've arranged the dresses so no problem. I tried mine in London and they've delivered it to the Cirencester branch."

"And there is one more thing," Ellie said smiling at her. "I was hoping you could help make the cake, I know it seems late in the day but I didn't want anything too fancy."

"Of course," said Marie. "I've always enjoyed baking with you and Jessica so this will be really special."

"Not with me," said Ellie. "I've asked Adam to do it as Pat's away but I would really like it if you could help him."

"With Adam," she said sounding surprised. "Does he

make cakes?"

"He's very good," said Ellie. "I was quite surprised too since it's not exactly his profession, but he's been a real godsend for Jessica and Edward. Shame he's not staying."

"Oh, what is his profession?" she said. She tried to keep the annoyance out of her voice, she really didn't want to work with a man she found quite rude.

"He's a photographer, well he was until he had to move back here. He's taking the photos at the wedding," said Ellie.

They reached the end of the walkway and followed the path through Silk Wood.

"Come on James," said Ellie. "Let's go look at these trees."

She led him off the path to explore for hidden treasures. He let go of Ellie's hand and ran ahead, Ellie followed close behind.

Marie pushed the empty pushchair along the path, she stopped and looked at her sister. "I've been offered a promotion," Marie said quietly.

"That's great," said Jessica. "You deserve it."

"There's just one thing," said Marie looking directly at her sister. "It's in Copenhagen."

"Copenhagen," said Jessica raising her voice. "You can't go there, we'd never see you."

"Shhh," said Marie. "I don't want to tell Mum yet, not until after the wedding."

"But you can't move," said Jessica.

"I don't want to move but I do want the job," said Marie. "It'll bring a whole host of opportunities, the position I've been offered is a really good one. I'll get to manage a much bigger team and work with new clients."

"But it's miles away," said Jessica. "Don't you have other options, perhaps you could work for another agency."

"I could but this is what I've worked towards, what I've always wanted. I have to think things through though, you know, work out how often I can get back and make sure I find a place that's big enough so everyone can visit," said Marie. "I really do want to stay close to you and," she looked ahead towards Ellie and James, "that gorgeous nephew of mine. But I love my job too."

"James will really miss you," said Jessica. "There must be other options."

"And what are you two whispering about?" Ellie said. Jessica and Marie had caught up with their mum and James who was happily playing hide and seek in the trees.

"Just sister stuff," said Marie looking a bit sheepish.

"Time for coffee I think," said Ellie. "I think this little man has worked up quite a thirst." She held James' hand and led them to the small cafe.

They found a table outside in a shady spot. Jessica strapped James into a highchair and put a dish of chopped fruit in front of him.

"Cake," he said pointing to the Victoria sponge in front of Marie.

Marie cut a small piece and gave it to James.

"You're going to spoil him," said Jessica.

"I know," said Marie winking at James. "That's my job."

3

Marie hadn't slept well and had woken before the alarm. She was worried that Jessica was upset about her move. This was the first time she'd spoken to anyone about her career choices before she'd started a job, she'd usually just ring and tell her sister and mum all about her new role. This time it seemed important to tell them about it before she left, ringing from Denmark after she'd moved didn't seem quite right somehow. However, right now she had to focus on the day ahead. She was up, dressed and ready to go. There were only a few days until the wedding and, even if everything was under control, there was still a lot to do. She knocked on Jessica's bedroom door.

"Come on Jessica," said Marie. "Our fitting is in ten minutes, I know it's just up the road but we are going to be late."

Jessica came out of the bedroom. "Sorry, just finding my shoes. I'm ready now," she said.

Edward was looking after James and had already taken him for a walk. Marie could hear Adam preparing food in the kitchen downstairs.

"When's Pat back?" asked Marie.

"End of the week, back for the wedding," said Jessica. "She's cut down her hours so we're going to have to find someone to replace her soon. And I'm not sure what Adam is going to do now that... well, I'm not sure he'll stay on for much longer. Look I know you're on holiday but do you think you could help out a bit later? Edward has to pop out and I need to take James to get a haircut."

"Of course, though I'm not sure Adam will be keen to see me," said Jessica.

"You two will hit it off I'm sure," said Jessica tentatively. "Once you get to know each other."

"Maybe," said Marie, not sounding convinced. She always enjoyed helping out her mum and sister in the tea room even if at times she'd tried to avoid the washing up. But this was different. She'd be working with a man who clearly didn't like her even if they'd barely met.

Marie and Jessica headed into town. The cloudless sky allowed the temperature to rise, this unseasonal heatwave showed no sign of ending. They passed St John's church where their mum would be married on Saturday. The new stonework was beginning to mellow, it was still brighter than the original walls but it didn't look out of place. Marie always thought the church looked more like a cathedral, it was magnificent in both size and presence. It towered over the nearby buildings and looked proudly over the town it served.

Marie pushed against the shop door and a little bell rang. She smiled, it must be the thing around here, bells on doors. Ellie had chosen the dresses a few months ago, she'd tasked her twin daughters with giving her away and wanted them to look the part.

"Morning," said the assistant. "I'm Jenny. This is the first time I've sold dresses to two daughters giving away the bride."

Marie smiled. "I know it's unusual but that's what Mum wanted so here we are," she said. "We feel quite honoured."

"It is a little odd though," said Jessica.

"I would have thought breaking with tradition would be right up your street," said Marie grinning at her.

"No, I mean being asked to give someone away. It's not like we're actually giving her to someone else. More like sharing I think," said Jessica.

"I've never thought about it," said Marie. "But you're right."

"Well I think it's lovely," said Jenny. "I've got the dresses ready so if you could put them on, don't worry about doing them up, I can do that for you, and I can see if we need to make any small adjustments, just to make sure they're a perfect fit."

"There's not much time left," said Jessica. "I hope they don't need too much work."

"They won't, and I've allocated the time so they'll be

ready," said Jenny. "The dresses are already hanging in the dressing room."

Marie went into the dressing room first and closed the door behind her. She touched the silk fabric. These were her mother's choice but they'd all agreed they were beautiful. She carefully slipped the dress on. Marie looked at herself in the mirror. The emerald green suited her skin colour and highlighted the flecks of green in her eyes. She pulled the material in at the zipper, the dress pinched in at her waist and then hung snugly over her hips.

She went into the fitting room. Jenny did up Marie's zip and buttons. She adjusted the short sleeves and pulled the dress down a little.

"This is a good fit but I think we can take it in a little more at the waist," Jenny said. She pulled the dress in at the back. "What do you think?"

Marie looked in the mirror, she'd never really thought about having clothes adjusted to fit her better. Off the peg had always seemed fine. But she had to admit that even this small change made a big difference.

"Yes, that would be great," she replied.

"And I would like to remove a little excess fabric from the back," she said.

"Sounds good," said Marie.

"You look stunning," said Jessica who had changed and joined her sister.

"We look stunning," said Marie.

Jenny made some notes, added a few pins and then unfastened Marie's dress before turning her attention to Jessica. She tugged at the zipper. She frowned briefly.

Jessica looked in the mirror. "It's too tight," said Jessica. "I don't get it, I've been the same size for months. I've even been to the gym to make sure I lost any remaining baby bulges."

Marie looked at her sister. The dress did look a little tight around her waist and the fabric bunched up a little. "Don't worry, you know sizes can vary," said Marie.

"I know, but I came in to try for size before we ordered them," said Jessica. Tears were filling her eyes.

"It's not a problem," said Jenny. "Wedding stress and all that often has an effect, I'm always taking clothes in or letting them out in the days before."

"But we've only got a few days left," said Jessica.

Jenny was at her computer. "I can get a size up delivered for this afternoon," said Jenny. "If you can come back first thing in the morning so I can fit the dress. It will definitely need taking in, you may have a grown a little but it is only a little." Jenny undid the zip and buttons.

Jessica wiped the tears from her face and headed for the dressing room. She nodded.

Marie looked at Jenny. "Tomorrow will be fine," Marie said. "We have to bring the youngsters into town to collect their clothes so we can come after that."

"Excellent," said Jenny.

Marie walked back to the tea room with her sister. Jessica was very quiet.

4

After the fitting Marie had an early lunch with Jessica and James before changing her clothes ready to help Adam in the tea room. She hadn't thought to bring working clothes so she had to make do with a pair of navy trousers and a cream and blue floral top. Not quite the usual black and white but it would have to do.

She headed into the tea room and grabbed a white apron. She was tying it around her waist when Adam walked out of the kitchen.

"Don't you have a plain top?" he asked frowning.

"No, I didn't bring one, I didn't realise I'd need it," said Marie feeling a little frustrated at him. She was here to help after all.

"Jo can show you the ropes, we're about to hit the lunchtime rush so you'll need to be a quick learner," he said indicating to a young girl who was taking an order from a couple.

Marie remembered Jo. She worked shifts that fitted around her college lectures. She must be in her last year by now. Marie decided she'd catch up with her later, see what her plans were for the future. She smiled at her.

"I think I can manage," said Marie sounding even more irritated. Adam had already headed back into the kitchen.

The lunchtime customers had started to arrive. Marie had not had a chance to look at the menu but she could soon see that the changes Jessica and Edward had made had gone down well. They'd really made the most of introducing new breads from the local bakery. The customers could choose a sandwich filling on a bread of their choice. They had olive, sun-dried tomato, cheese, beetroot, as well as a range of wholemeal and white breads. Customers could also choose to have a selection of breads with dipping oils and a salad. They still had the different teas and homemade cakes, she guessed Adam must be baking these whilst Pat was away. She smiled as she thought of how well Jessica had introduced her own personality without losing anything their mum had developed. She took her first order and headed towards the kitchen.

"Come on," said Adam. "Stop daydreaming."

Marie scowled at him and handed him the slip.

Marie had taken several orders when Adam called to say table six was ready. She picked up two plates from the kitchen table and headed into the tea room. She set the plates down. "Enjoy your meal," she said to the young couple.

"Excuse me," the girl said. "This isn't what we ordered."

Jo came over and picked up the plates. "Don't worry," she said looking at Marie and smiling. "These are for table six."

"But I thought this was table six," said Marie looking a bit confused.

Adam called from the kitchen again. She went back and picked up two more plates.

"Table nine," he said. "Are you sure you can find it?"

"I do know my way around," she said with gritted teeth.

"It's the second table after the door," he said. He had his back to her.

The table numbers had obviously changed, and she'd better learn them quickly before Adam found any more fault with her. She couldn't quite see why Jessica thought he was so good. Yes, the food looked great and she'd overheard customers complimenting him, but he was downright rude - at least to her.

Marie took the plates out. This time she wasn't taking any chances. "Two tuna and sweetcorn sandwiches," she said when she reached the table. She smiled at the two ladies.

"Yes please," one of the ladies said. "We've been looking forward to eating here, this tea room was recommended so we had to give it a go."

"Have you come far?" Marie asked as she placed the plates down in front of the customers.

"Dorset," one lady replied.

"Also a beautiful place. Enjoy your lunch," Marie said.

"And enjoy the rest of your stay." She smiled at them before heading back towards the kitchen.

"Table three," Adam shouted from the kitchen.

Marie quickened her pace.

"Table three," Adam said again as he stood in the doorway holding two plates.

"I'm coming," Marie said as she took the plates from him.

Marie spent the next hour almost running back and forth taking orders, delivering food and clearing tables for the next customers who seemed to be coming in a continuous stream.

"Excuse me," said a man on one of the tables. "Could we order coffee with our lunch? Sorry, I forgot to ask before."

"Of course," said Marie. She wrote down their order.

She looked around for the Jo, she was taking an order for a table of six. She had no choice but to do this herself.

She went to the coffee machine and picked up two cups. She looked at the new machine, she had never used this coffee machine before and there was not a list of instructions to follow. She looked again for Jo, she was still busy describing the different breads. She had no choice, she was going to have to ask Adam for help. She went into the kitchen.

"I have an order for two coffees," she said quietly, "and I've never used the machine before."

The man shook his head and followed her out of the kitchen.

Marie watched as he effortlessly made two impressive looking cappuccinos with a sprinkle of chocolate.

"Don't spill them," he said as he headed back to the kitchen.

Jo came back with an order. "Don't worry," she said. "He just takes a bit of getting used to."

Marie smiled and nodded. "I'm not sure I want to," she said under her breath.

5

How can it be morning already Marie thought to herself as she was woken by a knock on the bedroom door. She pulled the quilt over her face to block out the sunlight that had fallen onto her face. The previous evening she'd felt exhausted after working in the tea room. She'd played with James, bathed him and read him a bedtime story before having an early night herself. She wondered how Jessica managed all this, the tea room was enough work on its own let alone looking after a toddler as well. She'd never really thought about having children. At the moment she was single and liked it that way because she could concentrate on her work but maybe, in the future. As she'd thought about her future she'd started to doze, she'd slept until she heard the knock.

"Morning," said Edward as he opened the door slowly. "Tea and toast."

Marie pushed the quilt back from her face, opened her eyes and slowly pulled herself into a sitting position. If she had to wake up early then this was the way to start the day she thought. Jessica and Edward were really looking after her. Even though she wouldn't have minded James jumping on her bed in the morning they'd insisted that he wait for her to get up, she could hear him in the kitchen asking where she was.

Marie enjoyed having breakfast in bed, this was something that rarely happened, a consequence of living on her own. It was a good half hour before she was up and ready for the next set of tasks. Today she had to take James and Grace to try on and collect their wedding outfits. She'd only met Grace once in the last year, her walking had improved considerably, and Mum had said she was pretty much doing everything a young girl should be doing. She danced, took horse riding lessons and had even entered the school's athletics challenge. She frowned a little as she remembered that today she also had to make a wedding cake with Adam. She replaced the frown with as grin as she walked into the kitchen.

"Come here," she said to James as he ran towards her. She picked him up and planted a kiss on his head.

"Are we ready?" she said looking at Jessica.

"Ready as we'll ever be," replied Jessica.

Marie carried James downstairs and strapped him into his pushchair. He sat still allowing her to connect all the straps correctly.

"You're a natural," said Jessica. "He never sits still for me."

"He's only good for me because I'm not around that much," said Marie. "Can I push?"

"Of course. Reminds me of when we were younger and used to fight over who got to push the supermarket trolley, I'm sure mum always let you push," said Jessica.

"That's not the way I remember it," said Marie laughing. "You look a bit tired, are you okay?"

"Yes, just a lot of running around these past few days," said Jessica. "And I'm still embarrassed about yesterday, I'm not sure I can face Jenny again."

"It'll be fine," said Marie. "After we've collected the kid's outfits Mum's taking James and Grace back with her. That means we get an hour or two to have a wander round the shops and maybe have lunch."

"That'll be nice," said Jessica. "We still haven't chatted properly about your job."

"Over lunch," she said. "It'll be good to talk to you about it."

They headed to the wedding shop, a little place in a pretty courtyard. The window display included two white wedding dresses, one adult bridesmaid dress, two small bridesmaid dresses and also a pageboy outfit. Marie loved looking in this shop window, not because she wanted to get married but because she liked the thought of wearing a dress as gorgeous as these. She opened the door and manoeuvred the pushchair into the shop. Mum and Grace were already inside.

"Hi, Grace," Marie said smiling at the young girl sat on the sofa. "Are you excited about being a bridesmaid?"

Grace gave a nervous smile and nodded. A few minutes later and Grace was in her dress - green with a cream sash. Grace paraded in front of the mirror, she gave a little twirl and grinned. It reminded Marie of when mum had brought her and Jessica princess dresses. She was Belle and Jessica was Sleeping Beauty. They'd kept them on all day and would have worn them everywhere if they could have got away with it. They'd both stood in front of Mum's bedroom mirror and paraded just like Grace.

"You look amazing," said Marie.

"Thank-you," said Grace still grinning.

James was less enthusiastic about trying on his clothes, at one point he even climbed back into his pushchair and pointed towards the door. Marie laughed and gently lifted him out. Eventually the clothes were carefully wrapped and Mum took the two children back to the tea room.

"Right come on," said Marie. "Coffee before that fitting."

"Okay but I need to pick up a bit of make-up first," said Jessica indicating towards the small department store on Market Place. "It'll only take a minute, I just need a new foundation and lipstick, I've nearly run out and I don't want to be down to the last drop on Saturday."

As they walked along Market Place Marie looked up at the buildings. Nearly all were large and impressive giving a sense of the wealth that had enabled this market town to grow. This was a wide road overlooked by the stone Georgian and Victorian buildings as well as the timber-framed Tudor hotel. Today many of these buildings were banks, coffee shops, jewellers, antique centres and a wide range of shops. There was a queue at the bus stop, probably people from the local area who had popped into town to shop or meet friends for a morning coffee. She thought this was still a vibrant town, it was visited by many tourists but it also had a large permanent community that lived and worked here throughout the year.

Marie glanced in a shop window and caught a glimpse of Jessica's reflection.

"You really do look quite tired," Marie said. "Are you sure you're not coming down with something."

"Don't say that," said Jessica frowning. "I'm fine. I'll try and get an early night though, just to make sure."

They entered the department store, it was a high street name but was very different from the stores in London. It ran across several buildings joined inside by doorways. There was a multitude of small rooms with counters, shelves and rails placed in alcoves, under the stairs and any other space that could be used for stock.

"I'm just going to have a look upstairs," said Marie.

She left Jessica talking to the sales assistant. She obviously knew her well as she overheard Jessica telling her about the wedding. Marie headed to the back of the building and up the stairs. She browsed the rails before heading back down to meet her sister.

"Jessica," Marie cried out as she reached the bottom of the stairs.

Jessica was sat on a chair sipping from a glass of water.

"It's all right," said Jessica. "I'm fine now." Jessica handed the glass back to the assistant and picked up her bag. "Let's get that coffee." She stood up and headed towards the door.

"Jessica," said Marie. "Wait, I'm quite worried about you. Shouldn't we head back home."

"No. I really do feel fine now," said Jessica smiling at her sister. "I just felt a bit faint, too much rushing about I expect."

Jessica did actually look a lot better than earlier, she had some colour in her face and seemed brighter. They crossed the road and walked towards the coffee shop.

"Jessica," said Marie cautiously. "This might sound a daft question but," she paused, "could you be pregnant?"

"No, definitely not," said Jessica. She quickened her step as if to prove a point.

"Gaining a few inches, feeling faint, tiredness, there

could be lots of reasons, but, well…," said Marie.

"We haven't planned to have another just yet," said Jessica looking horrified.

"You may not have planned it, but could you be?" asked Marie again.

"I don't know," said Jessica. "No, I don't think I am."

"I think you need to find out," said Marie. "Book an appointment."

"If it'll make you happy I'll do a test." Jessica said. "The chemist is just around the corner."

"What now?" said Marie sounding surprised.

"No time like the present," said Jessica. "Just to put your mind at rest."

Jessica picked up her pace again and turned into Cricklade Street. The pavement here was narrow and uneven. Marie, like most people, walked in the road. It wasn't entirely pedestrianised but few vehicles came this way, and those that did had to slow down.

"Come on," said Jessica. "We can get the test then have that coffee."

Marie followed Jessica into the pharmacy and watched her buy a pregnancy test, she noted it was single test so she guessed Jessica thought she wouldn't need to double check. As soon as she'd paid Jessica made straight for the coffee shop and sat in a window seat.

"Slow down," said Marie. "We've got a couple of hours."

Marie ordered two cappuccinos. As she stood waiting at the counter she watched Jessica twist the edge of her t-shirt. She looked nervous, unsettled.

"I bought us cake as well," Marie said as she put the tray on the table.

"Let's get this over with," Jessica said. She picked up her handbag and stood up.

"You can't do it here," said Marie.

"Why not?" said Jessica. "Now you've put the thought in my head I need to find out." She headed towards the toilet.

"I get that but wait till we get home," said Marie.

"It'll only take a minute," Jessica called across the room. She turned and grinned. "Or two."

A few minutes later Jessica returned. She picked up her coffee cup and took a sip.

"Well?" said Marie when she returned.

"I have to wait two minutes," Jessica said looking down at her bag. "Order another coffee then I'll check."

Marie bought two more coffees and put them on the table. It looked like Jessica had been dissecting her cake, she hadn't eaten much of it.

"Well?" she said again.

Jessica opened her handbag and looked inside. Marie watched as Jessica started to shake.

"It can't be right," said Jessica.

"Tell me," said Marie.

"It says positive, but that can't be right," said Jessica. "What am I going to tell Edward."

"That you're expecting a baby," said Marie smiling at her and reaching across the table to hold her hand.

6

The rest of the day had gone by in a blur. After coffee Marie and Jessica had headed for the dress shop. Thankfully the dress needed quite a bit of taking in which cheered up Jessica no end. Her waistline had increased, but not by much, there were no obvious signs of the pregnancy yet. Jenny had assured them the dress would be ready in time. After a quick lunch they'd headed back to the tea room. Marie had helped Jessica look after James whilst Edward served the customers. She could hear them closing up. Now she had to help Adam make a cake. He was giving up his evening to help out but Marie couldn't help feeling a bit annoyed she had to work with him.

Marie headed downstairs. "Hi," she said a little tentatively as she walked into the kitchen. She was well aware that, for whatever reason, Adam did not like her.

"Your mum had a chat with me last week about what she'd like but obviously you know her better so how would you like to proceed," said Adam. He did not appear any friendlier this evening.

"I'm Marie by the way," Marie said.

"I know, your sister told me," Adam said curtly.

"And she told me your name is Adam," she said.

"Correct," Adam said. "Now the introductions are done shall we get on."

"Tell me your thoughts and then I can add anything I think important," Marie said. She was very aware that even though she'd knew her mother well they hadn't discussed the wedding cake so it was quite likely that Adam knew more about what her mum wanted than she did.

"Your mum said something simple and light so I thought cupcakes," he said.

"A plate of cupcakes, that doesn't sound very wedding like," she said.

"Not just a plate of cupcakes," he said. He sighed and sounded a little impatient. "A tiered display of cupcakes with the top ones specially decorated for the bride and groom. The cakes would be different flavours - lemon, chocolate, coffee, vanilla - and then decorated." He spoke slowly, as if to a child who didn't quite understand what was being said.

Marie could feel herself getting irritated. The idea was actually a very good one and she knew her mum would love it, but Adam did not have to speak to her this way.

"Sounds an interesting idea," said Marie.

"If you've got any better ones I'm all ears." Adam said.

"No," said Marie. "I was just thinking it through."

"Well we'd best get started," he said. "I suggest we make all the cakes first and then decorate tomorrow. I think we need about two hundred."

"Two hundred cakes," Marie said sounding shocked.

"Well how many do you think?" he asked.

"I don't know," she said.

"Well your mum has invited close on a hundred people in total, fifty to the wedding and afternoon tea and then another fifty on top to the evening do. I know it's informal but two cakes each does not sound excessive."

"No, you're right," she said. She was playing catch-up and was annoyed that Adam seemed to have remembered all the details about the wedding.

"Right, well that's fifteen minutes gone so I suggest we get started," Adam said. "I'll mix the first batch whilst you turn on the ovens and get the tins ready."

Marie walked over to the ovens. She frowned and turned. "What temperature?" she asked.

The rest of the evening was quite manic, they mixed up batches of cake mixture, added different flavours, spooned it into the paper cake cases and baked them. The smell in the kitchen was amazing - a mixture of lemon and vanilla and chocolate and sweetness. The temperature in the kitchen was starting to rise from the ovens. Every now and again a buzzer went to remind her another batch was cooked. She was tempted to use a spoon and taste the mixture in the bowls but she thought this would only result in another curt comment from Adam so she did the washing up without so much as licking her fingers.

They barely spoke during the evening however Marie noticed that Adam was totally focussed on what he was doing, he clearly cared about doing a good job and took his time weighing all the ingredients, whisking the mixture until he was happy with the consistency and putting just the right amount into each of the cake cases. She wondered what Adam had in mind for the decorations; she might as well ask.

"How are you thinking of finishing these cakes?" she asked.

He kept his voice matter of fact. "Coloured butter icing, I thought some white or cream with others the emerald green your mum has chosen. And then some sugar paper flakes to look like confetti, again I've got green and cream," he said.

"You've given this a lot of thought," she said. She felt a little irritated that he'd obviously planned exactly what he was going to do without consulting anyone and she guessed he would have not taken any of her ideas on board - not that she had any. To be fair it did sound amazing.

"Someone had to," he said. "The wedding's in a few days and everything had to be ordered."

The buzzer went off on the oven. Marie picked up a tea towel, opened the oven door and grabbed the two trays of nicely risen cakes. As she grabbed the trays the tea towel slipped from her hand. The heat caused her to step back taking the trays with her. They both hit the floor. Nothing was salvageable. There was just a crumbled mess of chocolate cake.

"What are you doing?" Adam said. "As if we haven't got enough to do."

Marie headed for the sink and held her hand under running cold water. She could feel the tears welling up in her eyes. Not from the burn, which didn't seem too bad, but from Adam's constant irritation with her.

"What do you think I'm doing?" she retorted equally short.

"Let me look at that," he said, his voice sounding a little softer.

"No need, it's not that bad," she said.

"All the same," he said.

"It's fine," she said.

"Okay, I'll clean up then mix up another batch," he said.

She turned around to look at him. "What is your problem with me?" she said. "My sister tells me how good you are and yet you've been rude to me from the moment I walked through the door." She heard her voice getting a little louder.

Adam stood up. "I'm sorry," he said. "I didn't mean to take it out on you. It's just I'm a bit... preoccupied at the moment and you represent, I don't know. Look I am sorry."

"So what's happened that you have to behave so badly?" she asked. "To me especially."

"It's complicated," he said. "I know that's not an excuse but things have not gone as planned for the last few months."

"And that's my fault?" she said.

"No," he said. "But I guess I'm a little envious of you and what you have."

"That doesn't make any sense," she said.

"I know. If you want me to finish the cakes then that's fine," he said sounding a little apologetic.

"No, my hand's fine," she said. "I'll finish cleaning up the mess and you can start mixing another batch."

They spent the rest of the evening working quietly. By ten o'clock two hundred and sixteen cupcakes were cooling on the worktops.

"Same time tomorrow," Marie said with half a smile on her face.

"Same time tomorrow," Adam replied. He didn't look at her as he spoke.

7

Marie looked at her reflection in her dressing table mirror. The morning sun provided just the right amount of light to do her make-up and style her hair. As she combed her hair she noticed the slight redness on her hand. The burn wasn't sore and would disappear completely in a day or two, but it did remind her of the previous evening spent making cakes with Adam. She frowned. Tonight she had to spend another evening with him, his manner towards her may have softened a little last night but she wasn't convinced that would last.

She continued to examine the reflection staring back at her. She hadn't yet put her make-up on but she still looked like someone who could take on any challenge, she even felt like she could, and yet, when she thought about her new job, there was a little niggle. She'd be leaving Jessica and her mum and, right now, Jessica needed her. She hadn't seen Jessica last night, it had been late when she'd finished making the cakes and it was all quiet when she'd finally gone upstairs. It seemed that she would have to formally accept the job before having a chance to reassure her sister.

With make-up applied and hair styled Marie put on her dressing gown and wandered into the kitchen. James was in his high chair eating cereal. As soon as he saw Marie James put up his arms to be lifted out. Marie sat beside him and planted a kiss on top of his head.

"Finish your breakfast first," she said ruffling his hair.

Marie looked across the table, Jessica was holding a tea towel that she'd twisted so hard there was a risk she'd actually tear it. Edward had his arm around her.

"Have I missed something?" said Marie.

Jessica looked at her and smiled. "I told Edward about the baby," she said.

Marie looked at Edward.

"Can you believe it," said Edward. "She apologised for being pregnant, thought I'd be really annoyed." He smiled at

Jessica and shook his head. "Well I couldn't be happier. I've been thinking for a while that it would be nice for James to have a little brother or sister but didn't dare mention it because Jessica already has enough on her plate."

"I am worried about how I'm going to cope," said Jessica.

"The point is," Edward said looking at Jessica, "you don't have to do everything on your own. We already know we have to employ more staff so start putting your feet up a little more often."

"Congratulations," said Marie. "And Edward's right, you do a fantastic job, but you don't have to do everything all at once. Some things can wait a day or two." She smiled at her sister.

"There's just one thing though, "said Jessica. "We've decided not to tell Mum until after the wedding. Don't want her worrying."

"Well that's only a few days away so I guess I can keep a secret until then," Marie said.

"Did you get the cake done?" asked Edward.

"Cakes plural," she said. "We've got to decorate them tonight."

"Sounds intriguing," said Jessica. "What are you doing, a multi-tiered creation?"

"I don't know if I'm allowed to say," said Marie. "I still don't think Adam likes me very much and I don't want to give him any more reason to shout at me."

"Don't be daft," said Jessica. "He's been a real asset. Just a shame he won't be staying."

"Why?" asked Marie.

"He's an excellent chef, could work in a proper restaurant, but that not what his real job is, or was," said Jessica.

"Mum said he's a photographer," said Marie.

"Yes, as you know he's doing the wedding photos, although that's not his usual thing. He had his own studio doing mostly photos for advertising and glossy magazines.

He's even had work on billboards," Jessica said. "Perhaps you came across him, he was based in London."

"No, never met him," said Marie. "Not that I remember, but then I don't work directly with the photographers. So what's he doing here, sounds like he was pretty successful."

"He was," Edward said. "But his mum lived in Cirencester and she became ill. He struggled to juggle his work in London with being here to care for her, eventually he gave up his studio and moved up here. He took this job because we can be a bit flexible, both with his mum and if he was offered any photography work."

"How's his mum?" asked Marie.

"She died a few weeks back," said Jessica. "He's sorting out her affairs and then, well who knows, I guess he'll go back to London. He's a great chef but I think he's only happy when he's behind a lens."

"I think I've been a bit hard on him," said Marie. "I thought he was just rude."

"Don't worry, he doesn't talk much about his life. I guess you just made him think," said Jessica, "working in London and all that."

"So that's what he meant," said Marie thinking about how he'd said he was envious of her.

"About what?" asked Jessica.

"Nothing," said Marie. "Just talking to myself."

Marie turned to her nephew. "Look at you," she said. "I think you've put most of that breakfast on you face."

James gurgled at her and attempted to get another spoonful of cereal into his mouth.

"Shall I take him and give him a bath?" said Marie.

"Please do," said Edward.

"And congratulations again," Marie said smiling at them both.

8

Marie had spent the rest of the day helping Edward and Jessica in the tea room. Adam had the day off. She enjoyed herself and even managed to master the coffee machine. By the evening she was tired but happy, only two days to the wedding, she was starting to feel excited. She had just finished tidying the tea room and getting it ready for the next day when Adam arrived.

"Hi," she said a little tentatively. Now she knew about Adam's situation she felt a little guilty about thinking badly of him.

"Hi," he replied heading for the kitchen. He wasn't exactly smiling but he did sound a little friendlier.

Marie decided to speak to Adam right away, tell that she knew about his mum, rather than tip-toeing around him and letting it slip by accident. The worst that could happen was he'd tell her to mind her own business and they'd spend the evening decorating cakes in silence.

"I heard about your mum, I'm sorry, it must have been hard for you," said Marie.

"I was, it not something I want to talk about," Adam said. He picked up a pack of butter from the table and squeezed it gently. He nodded.

Marie was glad she'd remembered to take the butter out of the fridge. She'd had experience of trying to soften butter in the microwave and it had never ended well. Her butter always went straight from hard to an oily liquid, there was no in between just soft stage.

Adam added the softened butter and icing sugar to a bowl and started to beat the butter icing, he then added a small amount of emerald green colouring.

"Mum will really be pleased," Marie said. "That green has sort of become the official colour for the wedding."

"I hope she likes it. I wish Pat was here though, she makes wonderful cakes," said Adam continuing to beat the mixture. The green dispersed in the mixture and gradually went from a marbled effect to an even colour.

"I know, but you do a pretty good job yourself," she said. "Where did you learn to cook? You approach it like someone who's been trained."

"It was a very long time ago, when I was at college, like most people I took a job in a restaurant. One evening they were short staffed in the kitchen and I helped out. Three years later I was still there. I learnt a lot," he said.

"Didn't you think of taking it up professionally," she said.

"No," he said shaking his head. "It was always a means to an end. The hours fitted in with my studies but as soon as I finished college I wanted nothing else than to be a photographer."

"And now?" she asked.

"Nothing's changed. This job is a means to an end. Jessica and Edward knew that when they took me on," he said sounding quite matter of fact. "Now that, well now mum's gone I can move back to London and start over. I've been away for quite a while but I've still got some contacts so who knows. You're from London aren't you?"

"Yes," she replied.

"Good job? Doing something you love?" he asked.

This was the friendliest the man had been since she'd met him. His voice was still monotone but at least he wasn't shouting at her.

"Yes, well at the moment, but that's about to change," she said.

"How come?" he asked.

She lowered her voice, she was about to share something she hadn't yet told her mum.

"I'm about to start a new job but I'm not sure now is the right time for a change," she said.

"But surely the business we're in is all about change," he said.

"It is," she said, "and I thrive on it. But, well, look I

haven't mentioned this to mum yet, not with the wedding and all that, but I've been offered a really great promotion."

"Sounds good to me," Adam said.

"The job's great but it would mean relocation," she said. "Copenhagen."

"Still can't see the problem," he said. Adam shrugged his shoulders.

"I know it's not the other side of the world but it would be a lot further away from Jessica and Mum," she said.

"Is that important?" he asked.

Marie thought about this for a moment. She'd always been close enough to her family to easily get together even if the reality was that this was only two or three times a year. But this job would mean she probably couldn't get back quickly if Jessica needed her. She paused. "Yes," she said after a few moments. "Right now Jessica needs me."

"Then don't take the job," Adam said, "it's your choice."

When he put it like that it sounded simple, and yet it didn't feel simple. "And then what?" she asked. This was something she hadn't thought about at all.

"Stay in the job you have? Get another job?" Adam said, it sounded like a question. He was mixing up a second bowl of butter icing. "And don't kid yourself your hesitation is about Jessica. If you're having second thoughts it's because you have doubts about whether you want the job."

"Of course I want the job," said Marie. "I'm just not sure this is the right time to move."

"Then take it," said Adam. "Don't use Jessica as an excuse."

"I'm not using Jessica as…," Marie said. She had raised her voice and stopped abruptly as she didn't want to disturb Jessica upstairs. "I know that if I want to be near Jessica I can get another job but there are so many decisions to make."

"Such as?" he said.

"Where do I live?" she said. "If I was going to move closer to Jessica now is a good time to do it. I could look at Bristol to work, there are some good agencies there."

"What else?" he said.

"I don't know," she said. "I guess I need to decide on whether or not to move before thinking about anything else."

"You seemed to have missed out one option," he said.

"What's that?" she said.

"Starting up on your own," he said. "Jessica says you are very good at what you do."

Marie laughed.

"Jessica also said you're very good at what you do," Marie said. "She was surprised I hadn't heard of you."

"London's a big place," said Adam.

"You ran your own studio, didn't you?" she said. "Will you go back to that?"

"It sounds like you're avoiding the question," Adam said. "Yes, I'll go back to photography, but I'll have to build up the business again. Renting somewhere in London is getting more expensive, I'm not sure I'll get enough work quickly enough to justify it. But I can pick up jobs here and there," he said.

"Why does it have to be London?" she asked.

"Everyone's in London," he said.

"Like you said, things change," she said.

"Maybe, but I don't know anywhere else," he said.

"You know here," she said.

"I don't want to be stuck doing weddings and family portraits," he said.

Marie frowned. "Is that so bad?" she said.

"Not if that's what you want to do, or if it's for friends" he said. "But it's not for me."

"So what's stopping you doing what you want to do somewhere else?" Marie asked.

"As I said, everyone's in London," he replied.

"Everyone?" Marie asked.

"Well maybe not everyone," he said.

"Sounds like you have as much thinking to do as I have," Marie said.

Adam frowned. "I think we need to get back to these cakes if we're going to get them finished," he said. "And like you said, nothing else until after the wedding."

Marie spent the rest of the evening helping Adam decorate over two hundred cupcakes. He showed her how to make the icing, ice the cakes and arrange them on the stands. They made two tiered stands of one hundred cakes each. Mixing the different shades of emerald green with the cream. They stood back to admire their work.

"These look amazing, just like a traditional wedding cake but better," Marie said. "Mum will love it."

"I hope so, we'll add the sugar confetti on the day," Adam said.

There were a few cakes left over which Adam arranged on a plate. "Just in case," he said, smiling.

Marie picked one up and rearranged the cakes to hide the gap. "I have to try one," she said. "Just to make sure." She smiled at him before biting into the thick icing and soft sponge.

"Perfect," she said.

9

Marie was up before Edward and Jessica. She filled the kettle and put coffee into the cafetiere. Usually they had instant but today she thought she'd surprise her sister. As she waited for the kettle to boil she stretched her arms above her head. The past few days had taken their toll. She was used to getting up early and working well into the evening but the work this week had been different, more physical, more emotional.

As she poured the steaming coffee into the mugs Edward appeared with James.

"I was going to bring you coffee in bed," Marie said.

"Thanks," he said. "It's a lovely thought but James here rarely thinks having a lie in is a good idea. Still, one more day and then you and Jessica can relax."

"Not much more to do now," replied Marie as she put her mug on the table and picked up James.

"I am going to miss you," said Marie as she ruffled James' hair.

"You've got a few days before you go back," said Edward. "And I promise we will come up to London this summer, even if we have to close the tea room for the day."

"I can't see Jessica being happy with that," Marie said laughing. She realised that Edward didn't know about her new job.

"Maybe not but she's going to have to get used to it," said Edward. "Hopefully we will get more staff but if not…."

"And what exactly will I have to get used to?" asked Jessica as she joined them in the kitchen.

"Taking a bit of time out," said Edward smiling at her.

"Not much chance of that," said Jessica.

"At least you can take a bit of a break this morning," said Edward. "Go and get your dresses and I don't want to see you until lunchtime."

"But…," said Jessica.

"No, buts," said Edward firmly. "Take your coffee and

go and get ready." Edward took James from Marie. "You too," he said grinning.

An hour later and Marie and Jessica were walking through the town. It had been a glorious week and the weather looked like it was going to be great for the wedding. As they approach the dress shop Jessica stopped.

"I'm sorry I haven't had time to talk to you about, well you know, your work," said Jessica. "It's just been a bit strange this week. And I don't want Mum worrying about anything."

"Don't worry, it's not every day you discover you're pregnant," Marie said. "I should imagine you're still recovering from the shock. And as for Mum, she's never actually been worried. I think that's a role you've taken on."

"You're probably right," said Jessica. "But I just want everything to be perfect. She deserves it."

"I want that too, and it will be," Marie said. "Wedding in the church, all sorted. Afternoon tea at the tea room, all sorted. Evening do in the club - all sorted. The flowers, outfits and photographer - all sorted."

"Only just," said Jessica as they walked into the shop.

"Only just is fine, so stop fretting," Marie said. "When are you telling Mum about the baby?"

"I'm not sure," Jessica said. "Sometime after the wedding, next week maybe."

"Well don't leave it too long, these things have a habit of getting out and you don't want her to hear from someone else," said Marie.

"And when are you telling mum about your job?" Jessica said.

Marie grinned at her. "After the wedding sometime," she said.

They both laughed.

"Come on," said Jessica. "Adam's got the afternoon off so I need to help Edward. I know we are going to have to find some new staff soon but I haven't had time to think about it. Pat wants to become very part-time, and I can't blame her. And I'm sure Adam will head back to London. Things seem to be changing fast and I'm not sure I can keep up."

Marie put her hand on her sister's arm. "I'll give you a hand," she said. "Today anyway."

They went into the shop for the final fitting. The dresses looked stunning. Jessica's dress fitted her beautifully, it even showed off her waistline which she was surprised she still had.

"You can hardly tell us apart," said Marie. "I think we'll do mum proud."

****

Marie and Jessica arrived back to the tea room just before lunch. Marie paused briefly as the aroma of toasted teacakes greeted her. It was something she associated with winter; their mum had often made hot chocolate and toasted teacakes when they came home from school on a cold afternoon. She remembered how the smell of cinnamon, the slightly burnt edges of the buns and the sight of butter melting slowly always made her feel warm even before she'd taken a bite.

Adam came out of the kitchen with two plates of the teacakes and handed them to Edward. He turned to Marie.

"Marie, if you're free I'd like to show you something," said Adam. "I'm just about finished here for today."

"I'm sorry but I promised I'd help here," said Marie. "Another day?"

"It's okay," said Edward. "We can manage. We're closing straight after lunch to get ready for tomorrow."

Marie looked a little nervous. "If you're sure," she said.

"We're sure," said Jessica. "We've run you off your feet ever since you arrived."

"Give me fifteen minutes," said Marie looking at Adam. She wondered what he intended to show her. A few days ago he was barely speaking to her and now he wanted her company.

Marie followed Adam down Market Place. She'd walked the same route this morning, the road had become a lot busier. It looked like quite a few people were on their lunch breaks and were taking the opportunity to eat their sandwiches in the sun, mostly they appeared to be heading for the Abbey Grounds behind the church. Older children were still in school but quite a few toddlers were also heading to the grounds with their parents. Some were carrying little bags of breadcrumbs to feed the ducks. Maybe she'd take James on a picnic next week.

"Where are we going?" asked Marie.

Adam slowed his pace a little. "Here," he said.

He stopped in front of a building that had recently been converted into offices. Some of the offices had already been let; there was a sign with the names of a solicitor, an investment company and an accountant.

"Very smart," said Marie. "Are we going in?"

In reply Adam pushed open the door. "You made me think last night," he said.

"About what?" she said.

"About taking a chance, making a change," he said.

"And you found this place last night and arranged a viewing this morning," she said, "I'm impressed."

He laughed. This was the first time she'd seen him laugh.

"Not exactly," he said. "I've an old friend who has taken one of these spaces, he told me they still have a couple available. I didn't think much about it but after last night I thought I might as well take a look."

They walked into a large reception area with two black leather sofas, a glass side table and several large potted plants.

"The rent can't be cheap if all this has to be paid for," Marie said as she took it all in.

"It's not," said Adam. "First floor." He headed towards the stairs.

The staircase was as grand as the reception with wide stairs and polished wooden bannisters. At the top the galleried landing headed off both to the left and right. They headed right.

Adam took a set of keys out of his pocket. "I picked them up from the agent," he said in answer to Marie's puzzled look. He opened the door and went inside.

"The building has been converted well," Adam said as he walked into the room. "The outside is traditional, probably listed, but inside it has a stylish modern feel, this could be a good place to set up a studio."

"It's huge," said Marie as she followed Adam. Her voice echoed around. She didn't really know how much space was needed for a photography studio but she'd never imagined it was this much.

"It is," he said. "In fact it's too big for me. The landlord is happy for interior walls to be installed so it can be divided into smaller spaces but even after setting up a studio space, putting in storage for equipment and creating an office there's still too much space for me, and of course I'd be paying for that space."

"Won't they divide it," she said.

"Possibly, or I could find someone to share it with," he said.

"That could work," she said. "Shared spaces are all the rage at the moment."

"Yes, that's why I decided to take a look and thought you might like to see it too," Adam said. He grinned a little.

Marie almost laughed in surprise. "Are you thinking about sharing with me? Until you mentioned it last night I'd never even considered setting up on my own," she said.

"Why not consider it now. You said you wanted to move on, or up, or something and you also want to be near your family. Maybe this is the solution," Adam said.

"That would be a massive step for me," she said still struggling with the idea that he'd even suggested it.

"Yes, but it sounds like you'd be taking a massive step anyway," he said. "I haven't made any decisions myself yet and we certainly don't have to share. I just thought it might be worth us both taking a look and considering our options."

"I wouldn't know where to start," she said. She walked towards one of the windows and looked out. This office was at the back of the building and overlooked a small garden area.

It had been landscaped and included a cobbled area with seating. The perimeter was made up of raised beds filled with a few architectural plants. She guessed the rent had to cover the upkeep of this as well.

"You know your business though," he said. "I'm not saying doing it for yourself is easy but you're more than halfway there."

"Maybe," she said. "This is a lovely building but I need to think about it, a lot."

"This space won't be around for long but there will be others," he said. "So take your time."

"Thanks," she said, "for bringing me."

Marie wandered back on her own leaving Adam to lock up and return the keys. Starting up her own agency sounded like an ideal next step but she'd never run her own business before and, despite what Adam said, she wasn't sure she had the skills. And even if she did have the skills she wasn't certain this was the right place to set up a new agency, after all it wasn't exactly London or even Bristol.

****

The tea room was closed when Marie arrived back. Jessica was clearing the tables so they could be set up for the wedding.

"Well," said Jessica. "How did it go?"

"How did what go?" said Marie. She didn't want to give too much away as she had no idea what she was going to do. She knew that if she told Jessica about the office she'd try to talk her into staying here and starting up a business. Marie needed time to think.

"Your afternoon," said Jessica sounding quite excited. She looked as if she was about to started jumping up and down.

"Fine," said Marie. "We had a wander and then coffee." The coffee bit wasn't exactly true.

"And that's it?" said Jessica.

"Adam just wanted a chat about what he was going to

do," said Marie. "You know, now he can move on. He just thought I might have some contacts." She smiled at her sister and headed upstairs.

10

The day of the wedding had finally arrived. Marie had set her alarm for five o'clock; this was earlier than she needed but she wanted to make sure that she had time to help Jessica as well get ready herself. The wedding was only nine hours away and there was the tea room to prepare, the food to check, although Jo and Pat were overseeing that, James to dress, hair to do. And now there was only eight hours and fifty-five minutes left. Perhaps Jessica's worry gene was catching.

She got out of bed and headed for the kitchen. She was surprised to see Edward already up and taking mugs from the cupboard.

"Coffee?" he asked.

"I was about to make you and Jessica one," she said. "I thought you'd still be in bed."

"I'll let you into a secret," he said. "I often sneak out of the bedroom before six and have a quiet cup of coffee before James wakes up. You know, a few minutes of calm before chaos ensues."

Marie laughed. "I have noticed that James is full of energy," she said. "I can imagine that can become quite tiring."

"It does," Edward said as he put the coffee in the mugs and poured in the boiling water, "but it's worth it."

"And soon there'll be two," said Marie as she took the mug from Edward.

"Yes," said Edward. "And I believe congratulations are in order for you too."

Marie looked at him a little puzzled. Jessica appeared at the door carrying James.

"Sorry," said Jessica. "I told Edward about your new job. Actually, what I said was that I didn't know how I was going to cope without you."

"You cope just fine," said Marie. "You should give yourself a bit of credit."

"Maybe," said Jessica. She put James into his highchair. He immediately turned to Marie and held out his arms. "And, as Edward pointed out to me last night, I need to be a little less selfish."

"I didn't use those words," said Edward, "I just said…."

"I know," said Jessica. "But I thought about it and realised I'd only been going on about how I'd miss you when I should have been congratulating you."

Edward looked up. "We're going to advertise for new staff next week and look at the rotas for both of us to make sure we have at least some free time," he said.

"I am going to miss you," said Jessica. "But I'm really proud of you, you deserve it. And we will come and visit all the time, it isn't that far after all."

"I'm really proud of you too, but Jessica…," said Marie. Before she could finish she heard a noise downstairs.

"That'll be Adam," said Edward. "He said he'd be in early to help get things ready but I didn't realise he meant this early. I'd better get down there and help."

"And I'd better get James fed," said Jessica.

Marie picked up her mug of coffee and headed back to the bedroom to get dressed. She could talk properly to Jessica later, or perhaps tomorrow.

****

Marie and Jessica arrived at the church in a white Mercedes, their mum was sat between them. The car was one of the few luxuries Ellie had agreed to. As they stood in the doorway of the church Marie took in the small bunches of white flowers tied at the end of the pews and noted the way the sunlight appeared to be sprinkled across the aisle as the windows turned the light from the summer sun into small patterns that danced across the floor.

Marie and Jessica stood either side of their mum. Ellie wore a knee length cream silk dress which fitted her beautifully. It was topped with an emerald green bolero. Her sandals matched her bolero. Her hair had been left loose and curled. She carried a simple bouquet of gypsophila, cream roses and green foliage. Marie looked at her mum and gently took her arm.

"This is it," said Marie smiling at her.

"You deserve this," said Jessica as she wiped a tear from her face. "This is your time now."

"I'll still be around you know," Ellie said turning first to Jessica and then to Marie. "I'll still be here for both of you."

"I know," said Marie. "And we'll always be here for you."

The music started and they all looked ahead. Michael was waiting at the end of the aisle.

James and Grace walked in front, everyone thought this was the safest option. James held onto Grace's hand and started walking slowly as soon as she gently tugged him. Although, as a small sign of rebellion, he had insisted on bringing his favourite toy plane.

When they reached the end of the aisle Marie and Jessica sat down with Grace and James leaving their mum stood beside Michael. Marie was glad she'd thought to bring tissues as small tears gathered in the corner of her eyes. It wasn't long before vows were exchanged, the register signed and the last hymn sung. Marie and Jessica followed their mum and Michael out into the Abbey Grounds ready for confetti and photographs.

Despite telling Marie that wedding photography wasn't his thing Adam clearly knew what he was doing. He expertly gathered groups of people together and took the standard shots before moving around the guests to take those ad hoc photos that captured the real moments. Marie caught sight of Margaret, a long-time customer of the tea room, she was chatting to Pat. It reminded her that time moves on and everything changes, sometimes in ways you don't expect. One way or another things were about to change for her.

It was over an hour before everyone headed back to the tea room. Marie noticed a few people taking photos of them as they paraded up the street. The temperature had risen considerably and most of the guests had taken off their jackets and ties. Mum would definitely have approved, as much as she liked tradition she didn't like people feeling they had to be on show, she wanted them to feel comfortable and relaxed.

Ellie and Michael walked into the tea room first to be greeted by Jo and Pat throwing more confetti. Marie gasped as she followed the newly married couple inside. The room wasn't quite finished when she had to leave Pat, Jo and Adam to it. Now the tables had all been dressed with cream tablecloths and green napkins. The top table was laid out nearest the window and long tables were set up at right angles to this. There were no place names, Ellie had insisted people could sit where they preferred. Food had been laid out on the tables in front of the counter with more in the kitchen ready to replenish the bowls as the afternoon wore on. In pride of place, sat on the counter, was the tiered plates of cupcakes Marie and Adam had made together. Now they were finished the arrangement looked stunning. The cream and emerald green butter icing looked simple but elegant. Marie had spent a few minutes with Adam earlier that morning perfecting the arrangement and adding the final decorations. The sprinkling of sugar paper confetti finished it all off beautifully. Many of the guests commented on how unusual the cake was. Adam was probably going to get a few requests to make more of these whether he liked it or not.

They took their seats and everyone helped themselves to the food. Marie sat next to Jessica who was sat next to Ellie. After an hour of eating, chatting and toasts Jessica looked first at Marie then her mum.

"Time for confessions I think," Jessica said.

"What have you two been up to?" asked Ellie looking at them suspiciously.

"Nothing really," said Jessica. "But we both have something to tell you. We didn't want to tell you before the wedding in case you worried."

"Jessica," said Ellie. "Whatever it is tell me right away

because now I am worried."

Jessica looked at Marie. "Go on," she said.

Marie shook her head. "You first," she said.

Jessica took a deep breath, leaned closer to her mum and whispered, "I'm pregnant."

"Jessica," said Ellie, "that's fantastic news." She hugged her daughter tightly.

"Shh," said Jessica. "We haven't told anyone yet."

Ellie lowered her voice. "When's it due," she asked.

"I've no idea," she said shrugging her shoulders. "We've only just found out."

"Well I thought I couldn't be happier today," said Ellie. "But this is," she looked across to the counter and laughed, "the icing on the cake."

Jessica turned to Marie. "Your turn," she said. She turned back to her mum. "This might not sound like good news but it is for Marie."

"What is it?" asked Ellie.

"I was offered a promotion, a really good one," said Marie.

"That fantastic," said Ellie. "What's so bad about that?"

"It's in Copenhagen," said Jessica. "We're not going to see much of her anymore."

Ellie smiled. "It might be a bit of a long journey but I'm sure we'll see just as much of you," said Ellie. "You deserve it." She reached along the table and took Marie's hand. "Well done."

"I turned it down," said Marie.

"You did what," said Jessica.

"I turned it down. I decided it was time to do something else," said Marie. "I wanted to tell you this morning but things got a bit too chaotic."

"Oh, Marie," said Jessica. "I hope this wasn't because of me. I know I didn't want you to go but I was just a bit scared with all this change and then finding out about the baby."

"No," said Marie. "I think I've had my doubts about this being the right move for a while now."

"You said it was time to do something else," said Ellie. "Do you know what?"

"Maybe," said Marie grinning. "Nothing's certain yet but I think I'll be starting up my own agency."

"In London?" asked Jessica. She too was grinning.

"In Cirencester," said Marie.

"When did you decide this?" said Jessica. "You never told me."

"I only decided yesterday afternoon," said Marie. "When I was out with Adam."

Ellie looked quizzically at Marie.

"It's a long story but we might share an office," said Marie. "And even if we don't I think I can make this work."

Ellie picked up her glass and raised it towards her daughters. "To a truly perfect day," she said.

Jessica and Marie raised their glasses.

"To changing times," said Jessica.

"And to new opportunities," said Marie.

The End

Other Books by Lily Wells

A Cornish Retreat

Cornwall seemed the ideal place for Lucy to get away and plan her future. Her fiancé had left her, she'd moved back in with her parents and her job didn't offer much in the way of prospects. If she was going to get her life back on track she needed a plan, and that plan didn't include starting a new relationship – until she met Jake. He appeared to be everything Lucy wanted – but could she really trust him?

The Cornish Cookery School
The Grand Opening

Alice has been left the Old Rectory by her Aunt Ruth. She'd loved spending her childhood summers in the large old house with its woodland and a secret path to the beach. These were happy times and the place held many good memories. Now the house looked tired, the garden was overgrown and the path to the beach was almost impassable.

Her parents are determined she should sell the house and concentrate her energies on her job in London, a job that doesn't bring her any joy. Alice has other plans, she intends to keep the house but has no idea what to do with it.

A chance meeting with local handyman Seb gives her an idea – turn the Old Rectory into a cookery school. But first she has to convince Seb to help her and he is less that keen.

Lily Wells

The Cornish Cookery School 2
The Autumn Fare

Alice has been running the cookery school for only a few weeks and already has bookings into the next year. Life seems pretty much perfect but not one to stop and enjoy the moment she is already thinking of new ways to promote and grow the business. One of her ideas is to organise an autumn food fare to give local people the opportunity to see what they offer. Her relationship with Seb is starting to develop into something more than a business arrangement however her parents have other plans for her love life when they make a surprise visit and bring along an old flame. They expect her to drop everything and entertain Michael with the hope that they will rekindle their old feelings for each other. Just as Alice thinks she's got everything under control an overnight storm threatens to ruin everything. Alice and Seb have only a few short hours to turn a mud bath of a lawn and a collapsed marquee into somewhere that showcases their cookery school and impresses her parents.

Christmas in Cornwall

Heather has planned the best Christmas ever. She is going to spend Christmas Day with Nick, they are going to commit to their relationship and, finally, she will be able to introduce him as her boyfriend.

One phone call from her sister and her plans are thrown into disarray when Heather has to hot foot it down to Cornwall to help Sarah look after the children. She loves spending time with her nephew and niece but is worried that Nick doesn't seem keen to answer her texts or phone calls. As long as she can get back home on Christmas Eve she should still be able to get her plans back on track.

Manufactured by Amazon.ca
Bolton, ON